A Candlelight Ecstasy Romance®

"YOU DECEIVED ME, ANNELISE. YOU'VE BEEN LYING TO ME FOR DAYS NOW!"

"That's not true. At least I didn't do it intentionally. I just needed some time. I would have told you everything eventually."

"When? After I'd spent all summer searching for those papers you had hidden in your drawer?"

"Trust doesn't come easily to me, Max. You've got to understand that."

"Oh, I do," he said, taking a threatening step toward her. "I understand that you don't mind making love with a man you don't even trust. And I understand that you don't mind telling a man that you love him just so he'll never suspect you're working against him all the time."

CANDLELIGHT ECSTASY CLASSIC ROMANCES

PRIVATE INTENTIONS

Saranne Dawson

A CANDLELIGHT ECSTASY ROMANCE®

Published by
Dell Publishing Co., Inc.
1 Dag Hammarskjold Plaza
New York, New York 10017

ISBN: 0-440-17147-4

Printed in the United States of America

September 1987

10 9 8 7 6 5 4 3 2 1

KRI

To Our Readers:

As of September 1987, Candlelight Romances will cease publication of Candlelight Ecstasies and Supremes. The editors of Candlelight would like to thank our readers for 20 years of loyalty and support. Providing quality romances has been a wonderful experience for us and one we will cherish. Again, from everyone at Candlelight, thank you!

Sincerely,

The Editors

"Robert Harrington wasn't a friend, Max. He was a colleague. I'm sure you can appreciate the difference. Harrington didn't really have any friends because he was vain and status-conscious and more interested in publicity than in science.

"Just before his disappearance, some of us thought that he might actually have become mentally unstable. His work was inferior and we all knew he'd never be granted tenure. But he said that he and Otto Vandeveldt were on the verge of a major breakthrough—'Nobel Prize magnitude,' he called it. And he also said that Vandeveldt was 'giving him some trouble.' "

"But surely the police must have questioned Vandeveldt when Harrington disappeared?" Max asked, and frowned.

"Oh, they did. I even talked to him myself. Vandeveldt said that he hadn't seen Harrington in months and denied any knowledge of a breakthrough."

"And that was the end of it?"

"Yes, because shortly thereafter, Harrington's car was found abandoned in New York City—hundreds of miles from Vandeveldt's home. And don't forget the obvious: no police officer—or anyone else, for that matter—is going to question the word of a Vandeveldt."

"But that's just what you want me to do," Max protested, liking this less and less.

"Not exactly. Otto Vandeveldt is dead, and to be honest about it, I'm less concerned with what happened to Harrington twenty years ago than I am with whether or not that breakthrough actually occurred. When you see these new papers of Harrington's, I think you'll understand."

CHAPTER ONE

"Otto was . . . a bit erratic, Dr. Armstrong, particularly toward the end of his life. To be quite candid about it, we were never certain that the work he claimed to be doing was of any value whatsoever." The slim, elegant middle-aged woman paused to smile self-deprecatingly, then went on.

"I have no way of knowing, of course, but it was my brother John's opinion that Otto had wasted his life. You see, Otto was the eldest of my three brothers, and the only one to show no interest in the family's businesses. John resented that. I'm afraid that our family is much like any other—full of sibling rivalries and long-standing grudges."

Max Armstrong suppressed a smile. The Vandeveldt family was scarcely "like any other," but if Hilde Vandeveldt Newcombe chose to believe that, it was really no concern of his. His concern was her late brother, the "erratic" Otto Vandeveldt.

"My research suggests that your brother might well have been on to something—that he might have been engaged in some truly seminal work in theoretical physics. As it happens, some of our interests coincide. Are his papers still in existence?"

Hilde nodded. "Oh, yes. After his death, my niece packed them all up and stored them in the attic. You see, Dr. Armstrong, Otto lived all his adult life at our family's summer home near Lake Champlain, and in his will, Otto specified that his papers should remain at Singing Waters."

"Singing Waters?" Max queried.

9

"That's the name of our summer home. Otto treasured its peace and quiet, and rarely left it. The rest of us gather there every August, but Otto made it his permanent home." She paused and then waved a bejeweled hand in a helpless gesture.

"There are boxes and boxes of papers, and as far as I know, they're in complete disarray. We did discuss the possibility of having someone look them over, but my brothers concluded that they were probably worthless."

"Well, I'd like to try my hand at it," Max said, hoping that he didn't sound overly eager. "That is, if you and your family would permit it. I could go there after the term ends and be gone well before your family arrives in August."

"I'm sure that no one would object, Dr. Armstrong. In fact, you'd be doing us all a favor. However, my niece will be spending the entire summer there, so I must check with her first."

Max thanked her and reiterated his interest in her late brother's work. After reading Harrington's newly discovered papers, Max—like his department head—had become convinced that, contrary to what Otto Vandeveldt had said, the two men had been breaking fresh ground.

That, of course, led quite naturally to the question of why Otto Vandeveldt would have lied. This had indeed become a very delicate matter. If their suspicions proved to be correct and Otto Vandeveldt was in some way connected with Harrington's disappearance, the Vandeveldt family would be anything but pleased. However, since Hilde hadn't turned him down, he assumed that if Otto *had* had anything to do with Harrington's disappearance, his family hadn't known about it or even suspected it.

Sipping thoughtfully at his drink, he wondered if that niece could pose any problems. What was she doing there all summer alone, anyway? From what Rowan, Hilde's husband and Max's friend, had told him, this Singing Waters was very isolated.

Somewhere in the back of his mind was a vague recollection of Hilde's having mentioned a niece before. He searched his memory, then came up with it. A year or so ago, Hilde had invited him to a dinner party to meet her niece, but the niece hadn't shown up. He remembered that Hilde had been very upset about it and had remarked that the girl was somewhat irresponsible. An artist, if he remembered correctly. Well, that could explain her being at Singing Waters for the summer. Max's acquaintance with artists was very limited, and he tended to regard them with considerable skepticism.

Several weeks later, after turning in the last of his grades and helping his graduate students set up their summer research projects, Max bade a grateful farewell to academia and drove northwest toward Lake Champlain. He knew he was going to be slowed down by the trailer with his dirt bike and the trip might take him two days, but he was determined to get some pleasure out of this business.

Max continued to have very mixed feelings about this whole affair. Generally speaking, he preferred to keep his two lives separate. From September to May, he was a theoretical physicist, tenured professor at MIT and member in highest standing of the academic community.

But from May to September, Max shed his academic skin and went exploring. He'd spent summers climbing in the Himalayas and the Alps, gone caving in the Pyrenees, and had once taken a harrowing trip down the Amazon.

These adventures provided, he thought, a nice counterbalance to his academic life. He explained it to bemused fellow faculty members as "giving his brain a rest"—something none of them could deny it deserved.

But work was intruding on part of this summer, and he resented that. Still, he'd seen no way out of it. Because of his own area of expertise and because of his acquaintance with a member of the Vandeveldt family, he was the logical choice. His curiosity *had* been piqued by those papers of Harrington's, but if it hadn't been for the stipulation in Otto Vandeveldt's will that the papers remain at Singing Waters, he would have let it go until fall and examined the papers at MIT.

11

It was late afternoon when he came to the old stone pillars that marked the entrance to Singing Waters. Between them was a wooden gate, freshly painted white. There were no signs of any kind, but Hilde's directions had seemed clear enough, so he stopped and got out to open the gate. He'd been driving for miles through green wilderness, and still more of the same stretched beyond the gate. Rowan had told him that the Vandeveldts owned more than a thousand acres here.

The gate was latched but not locked, so he drove through and then went back to close it, noting for the first time the electronic device attached to it. Probably it would warn anyone at the house of his arrival.

He began to wonder if he should have stopped in the village some miles back to call his hostess. Technically he was a day early, but he'd been deliberately vague about the time of his arrival, knowing that the trailer with the bike might slow him down. But it was too late to think about that now; he'd just have to take his chances.

He got back into his van and checked the odometer. According to Hilde's directions, it was almost four miles from the gate to the house. At slightly more than three miles, he crested a small hill and glimpsed a lake through the trees. Then the road descended again, crowded on both sides by the thick, dark forest, and the lake disappeared.

When the road rose again, the lake was spread out before him —but Max barely noticed it. His feet went automatically to the clutch and brake as he stared in utter astonishment. He supposed that he should have been expecting something like this, given the Vandeveldt wealth, but Singing Waters bore no resemblance to any summer home he'd ever seen. Except perhaps the fabled "cottages" at Newport.

The house was built of native stone and sat solidly to one side of the large lake, looking as though it had been there just as long. An enormous, many-gabled affair with a red-tiled roof, it boasted

12

three full stories and an attic. With a low whistle of appreciation, he eased the van forward.

Then, as he approached the house, he noticed a large boathouse and a raft anchored in the middle of the lake. There also appeared to be some sort of building half hidden in the woods on the far side of the house from the lake and something else to one side of that. He guessed that the larger building had once been a stable and carriage house and now served as a garage. The smaller building, just barely visible, was probably a caretaker's cottage.

Then he was at the circular end of the driveway, where he noticed the fountain for the first time. As large and elaborate as it was, it was still rendered insignificant by the massive house. When he came to a stop and shut off the van's engine, he realized immediately where this incredible place had gotten its name. In the utter stillness, the waters gurgled and dripped and did indeed seem to sing.

He got out of the van, still staring at the house. Long, leaded-glass windows stared blankly back at him from between their ivory-painted shutters. The large front door was painted ivory, too, and was surrounded by huge stone planters in which grew a profusion of summer flowers.

Max Armstrong, learned professor and intrepid explorer, was beginning to feel very much out of his element.

Annelise heard the gate buzzer only because it happened to sound in the thunderous silence between selections on her stereo. It would also be buzzing in the caretaker's cottage, but she wasn't sure if George and Mary were home at the moment.

When the next ear-shattering blast of heavy metal wiped it out, she went back to applying paint to canvas with a small trowel. Surely it wasn't that professor arriving early. Actually, she'd been hoping that he'd get himself hopelessly lost in the woods and give up. Academic types were notoriously inept when it came to dealing with life beyond ivy-covered walls.

Annelise had been very irritated by her aunt's call. Damn the woman anyway. Hilde knew perfectly well that she had come up here to prepare for her most important show yet. But then Hilde, who firmly believed that art had ceased to exist after the dawning of the twentieth century, had never taken her niece's work seriously.

"He's quite brilliant, my dear, and an absolute gentleman."

Annelise groaned as her aunt's words came back to her. Some recommendation *that* was. She didn't want to share Singing Waters with a "brilliant gentleman" or anyone else, for that matter. If she'd wanted company, she would have invited her own—and it certainly wouldn't be a stuffy professor with thick glasses, ill-fitting clothes and a perpetually distracted air.

Besides, she didn't want anyone pawing through Otto's papers. She'd been opposed to the earlier idea of hiring some graduate student to put them in order and determine their importance, and she'd won that battle. But now, instead of getting a kid whose judgment would have been suspect in any event, she was getting a full professor.

She'd already decided that if this Dr. Armstrong belittled her uncle's work, she was just going to toss him out—shabby tweeds, thick glasses, and all. Annelise had loved her uncle and her love had been returned in full measure. Unlike her cold, distant father, he'd always had time to listen to her ideas and help her with her problems.

Besides, Otto had been the family rebel of his generation and Annelise had clearly inherited his mantle. She had often thought of them as being two free spirits hopelessly surrounded by ponderous dullards. Therefore, she had no intention of listening to Maximilian Armstrong, PhD, telling her in supercilious tones that Otto had been a fraud, a description she'd certainly heard often enough from her late father.

She set down the trowel, deciding that she'd better see who was arriving. Running a hand through her hair in a futile attempt to restore order, she left her studio prepared to deal summarily with this intruder. It didn't seem likely that it would be the professor, since surely a "gentleman" would have called to inform her of his early arrival.

She ran down the broad, curved staircase, crossed the wide slate foyer, and flung open the front door.

Max was just approaching the front door when it opened to reveal one of the most incredible creatures he'd ever encountered. Already unbalanced by the fantastic house, he just gaped unabashedly at the girl who stood there.

Hilde Vandeveldt had hinted that she disapproved of her niece, and he now understood the woman's capacity for understatement. The creature who peered first at him and then at his van looked like something from the cover of a rock album. Max wasn't at all fond of rock music, and he could now hear just that pouring forth from somewhere in the vast interior of the house.

Surely he must have been mistaken in his assumption that this was the niece Hilde had once wanted him to meet. Not only was she far too young for him, but she was also about as far from his type of woman as it was possible to get.

She was dressed in a wrinkled, baggy, black outfit that reminded him of the clothing worn by practitioners of karate. Instead of the usual sash, however, she was wearing a gold-scaled snake. The snake was biting its own tail to hold it in place about her waist, and red gem eyes winked at him in the bright sunlight. Her feet, beneath the cropped pants, were bare and not very clean.

But despite this outlandish outfit, it was her hair that commanded his attention. It was very long, very thick and very black —with a swath of pure white running through its center and a narrow streak of bright red in the middle of that. A punk rocker: no doubt about it.

If it hadn't been for that obviously expensive snake belt and those deep blue eyes that reminded him of Hilde's, Max would never have believed that this apparition could be the daughter of one of the country's oldest and wealthiest families. He wasn't actually sure that he believed it even now.

"This is private property and we don't permit camping here," Annelise stated firmly. She had sized up the situation immediately, once she'd seen the van and trailer. It happened at least once or twice every summer because the family refused to put up a sign at the gate.

"Uh, are you Annelise Vandeveldt?" Max inquired politely. He'd heard that haughty and proprietorial tone and knew now that, incredible as it was, this must indeed be his hostess.

"Yes," the apparition answered with somewhat less certainty as she looked from the van back to him. Surely, she thought, *this* couldn't be the professor.

"Are you Dr. Armstrong?"

He nodded, suppressing a smile as he realized that he apparently wasn't what she'd expected, either. "I'm sorry to be arriving early and unannounced, but I'd expected the trailer to hold me up more than it did."

Annelise peered again at the trailer behind the gold and brown van. "What is that thing? I've never seen such an ugly motorcycle."

Max had to laugh. After her earlier imperiousness, this remark sounded far more in keeping with her outlandish appearance. "It's a dirt bike and it's utilitarian rather than beautiful. I thought I might put it to use while I'm here."

"I'm sure the deer and bears will love it," she said dryly. "There's a garage at the side of the house. Do you need help bringing in your things? Oh, welcome to Singing Waters, by the way," she added somewhat grudgingly.

He thanked her and assured her that he could manage, noting with amusement the return of that lady-of-the-manor tone. Then, just as he turned back to his van, a compactly built older man appeared.

"I was just going to call you, George," the woman said. "This is Professor Armstrong. Professor, this is our caretaker, George Whitney."

As he shook hands with the man, Max noted that his hostess's tone had warmed considerably when she spoke to the caretaker. Apparently the man met with her approval, although he suspected that he himself didn't.

Annelise continued to stand in the doorway, staring at this unlikely professor. She hadn't yet recovered completely from her shock. Instead of the anemic-looking, bespectacled type she'd expected, she had gotten a very vital and rugged-looking man clad in worn jeans and a light sweater that emphasized his long, lean body.

He was also far younger than she'd expected—probably in his mid-thirties. He was actually quite attractive in that healthy, outdoorsy sort of way: regular features, thick, slightly wavy brown hair and warm, dark eyes.

How on earth could someone who spent his life in musty classrooms and laboratories look like this?

He started back toward her then, hefting two large suitcases easily, and she noticed that he even had a small cleft in his chin. My God, she thought, the man looks like a walking cigarette ad. All he needs is a horse or some climbing rope wrapped around his shoulders.

She stepped back inside, and he strode past her, followed by George, who was carrying more of his things. At that point, she decided that, in addition to everything else that was wrong with him, he was also too tall. Annelise was barely five-four herself, and firmly believed that no person had a right to be more than five-ten. He topped that by at least three or four inches.

"We're putting Dr. Armstrong in the rear corner room, George," she said as she headed across the foyer to the staircase. Then, when she saw that the professor had stopped, she stopped, too.

He was staring about him in obvious bewilderment, and she found that strangely satisfying. No one could believe Singing Waters without seeing it. Even those with full knowledge of the family's legendary wealth were invariably unprepared for this summer home. Annelise knew, as they all did, that the place was a dinosaur. It was absurdly lavish and cost far too much to maintain, but she, like the rest of the family, loved every inch of it.

The wide slate foyer, with its vaulted ceiling and enormous silver and crystal chandelier, opened onto two large salons, both of which were furnished with pieces that were an antique dealer's dream.

Each room boasted a marble-manteled fireplace, upon which sat some of the rare clocks collected by a great-uncle, together with fine old silver pieces gathered by several other ancestors. The works of art that presently adorned the walls were of excellent quality, although the very best of them had been removed after Otto's death and now hung in other family homes or in museums.

"Some summer home," her guest finally said to her, grinning boyishly.

"Be it ever so humble," she quoted airily as she once again started up the staircase. She'd found that grin endearing, so she quickly adopted her very-proper-hostess voice again.

"I think you'll like your room. It's the nicest guest room. We all have our rooms in the family wing." She gestured to her right. "And your room is on the far end of the guest wing."

The distance between those rooms suddenly seemed absurdly important to Annelise. She didn't like this state of affairs one bit. Why couldn't Professor Max Armstrong be what he was supposed to be?

The rock music, just barely tolerable to Max until now, grew deafening as they proceeded down the hallway. She turned around in time to see her guest wincing and George smiling.

"Don't worry, Professor," she shouted above the din. "I'll keep it down. I only play it loud when I'm alone here, and besides, I don't usually work in the early mornings or at night."

Max managed a nod and a smile, and she thought she heard George chuckle. Leaving them for a moment, she went to her studio to turn the music down. She really had gotten carried away.

Then she crossed the hall to the guest room and found him

looking around appreciatively. She liked the fact that he didn't even try to hide his astonishment at Singing Waters' opulence. Too many guests had made ridiculous attempts to be blasé about the place.

"This is your bath," she said, crossing the large, sunny room to open a door on the far side. "The plumbing is disgustingly noisy, but it works well enough."

He came to the doorway and glanced in, filling entirely too much space. She slid past him self-consciously, holding herself as tall as possible.

George had set down his burdens and was about to leave. "Mary is baking some blueberry pies, Nellie. I don't suppose you would want one." His eyes twinkled mischievously.

Annelise made a face. "I gained five pounds up here last summer, George. Is she trying for ten this year?"

"I'll bring it over and leave it in the kitchen. Do you like blueberry pie, Dr. Armstrong?"

Max, who had been speculating about his hostess's figure, quickly shifted his gaze to the caretaker and grinned. "I've never been known to turn down homemade pie of any kind."

The older man chuckled. "I'll be going, then. I'd offer to put that van in the garage for you, but I don't know if I could handle the trailer."

Max followed the caretaker downstairs to take care of that chore himself, but his mind remained on his hostess. Her appearance hadn't shocked George, so he guessed that it must be normal for her. He smiled to himself over the unlikeliness of that nickname, Nellie. But then, everything about her was not just unlikely—it was damned near impossible. Away from her now, Max wasn't altogether sure that he hadn't just dreamed her.

When he returned to the house, she was nowhere to be seen, so he decided to go upstairs and unpack after pausing once more to stare in awe at his surroundings. The music was still playing, although at a more tolerable level now. Still, it clashed violently with the grandeur of the house—just as his hostess did, he thought, and chuckled.

He followed the music to its source and found her in the room just across from his bedroom. She was standing before a large canvas, slapping paint on it with a small trowel. The entire room, which must have once been a charming sunporch, was filled with paints and canvases. He cast an appreciative eye at the expensive stereo equipment in one corner, regretting that it wasn't being put to better use.

Her back was to him as she worked, and he watched her, trying to make some sense of the bold colors and strange forms. But art had just never interested him that much—although she certainly did. Standing as she was now, before the large canvas, she suddenly looked very tiny. Strange, but he hadn't noticed that before. Despite her small size, Annelise Vandeveldt had a tendency to fill up quite a lot of space.

It was virtually impossible to see her figure beneath those baggy pajamas, but he noticed now that the snake belt encircled a very tiny waist. He also saw that the white streak in her hair extended all the way down the back, while the red one stopped halfway down. Why, he wondered, would she want to make such a travesty of that glorious black hair?

He was just beginning to wonder about her age when she turned to put more paint on the trowel and saw him standing there in the doorway.

"I, ah, didn't know that artists worked with trowels," he said for lack of anything better to say.

"Oh, I've been known to paint with some very strange things at times—even my feet," Annelise replied airily, knowing that this man was already shocked and could probably be pushed a bit further in that direction.

"Don't worry, Dr. Armstrong, I won't bore you with my art if you won't bore me with your physics."

"It's Max, and I promise not to do that. Does everyone call you

20

Nellie?" He was unable to keep a trace of amusement out of his voice.

She heard it. "Only the family," she replied with cool formality.

"All right—Annelise it is, then. Is there any live-in staff here?" He was thinking that a place this size must be crawling with servants, even though he hadn't yet seen any.

She shook her head. "Not for years now. There's a gardener and a handyman who come in from the village. Mrs. Mayhew is the cook and housekeeper and two of her daughters help out as maids when needed. Only in August when the whole family is here do we usually need more help than that, and then we get them from the village, too. Mrs. M. and the girls come in three days a week. I do my own cooking. Can you cook?"

"After a fashion," he replied, thinking that the question was a subtle reminder that he wasn't exactly entitled to guest status. "I'm sure that I can manage, but I didn't bring any groceries with me."

She waved the trowel. "No problem. Just let Mrs. M. know what you want and she'll take care of it. There's a list tacked to the fridge. In the meantime, both the fridge and freezer are full. Fortunately for you, I've just gotten over a bout of vegetarianism. I decided to quit when I began to eye the deer that come down to drink out of the lake. So the freezer's full of steaks that I had sent up from Manhattan. If that will suit you for dinner, I'll just take another one out."

Max said that would be fine. A punk rocker who had her steaks flown in from Manhattan? Oh, there were undoubtedly even more interesting revelations to come. He was beginning to enjoy the prospect of sharing the house with her.

"I tend to eat at irregular hours when I'm working, but I'll make the supreme sacrifice and hold a sitdown dinner in your honor tonight, Professor. After that, you're on your own."

"Thank you," he replied with mock formality, inclining his

21

head slightly. "Now I won't bother you anymore if you'll just tell me where I can work."

"The library, I think. That's where Uncle Otto used to work. His papers are all up in the attic. I'll show you where tomorrow. Just go downstairs and keep turning right and you'll find the library eventually."

"How many rooms does this place have?" Max asked curiously.

"Thirty-four—not counting the attic and basement. We don't use the third floor much, though. The rooms up there are small—originally intended for servants, of course. Now they're used only for an overflow of guests."

"It's the most amazing house I've ever seen," Max said sincerely.

She smiled at him. "Yes, isn't it?"

Max took a tour of the first floor, feeling as though he were touring a museum. That anyone—even the Vandeveldts—could call such a place a summer home was unbelievable. Throughout the numerous rooms, there were silver and crystal chandeliers and wall sconces. The floors were covered in a rich variety of oriental rugs, and the furniture all had that wonderful patina of fine wood that has been lovingly cared for. Works of art adorned the walls, and tables and mantels were filled with clocks, vases, and figurines whose values he could only imagine. All of it was immaculate and in perfect repair, and Max estimated that the mere upkeep of this fabulous house probably exceeded his annual salary.

To someone who had grown up in a factory town in central Massachusetts, Singing Waters was a wilderness palace presided over at the moment by an alternately flaky and haughty princess.

Fortunately, he felt reasonably at home in the library, although even there, he wasn't able to forget where he was. It was a large room, richly paneled in dark wood and lined on two walls floor to ceiling with well-filled bookshelves. A third wall was broken by double doors that led to the terrace behind the house, and the fourth held a huge stone fireplace.

Near the fireplace was a handsome leather sofa and two matching chairs. In the far corner, at an angle to the bookshelves, was a big old mahogany desk with a deep leather chair. In another corner was a portable bar whose polished top gleamed with crystal decanters.

Max went to the desk and sank down into the deeply cushioned chair, inhaling the distinctive aroma of well-kept leather. Sitting there and surveying the room, he felt . . . well, almost baronial. Or, at the very least, rather like Alistair Cooke on *Masterpiece Theatre.*

The image of his improbable hostess lingered in his mind. She could very easily become a distraction he could ill afford. There was nothing really lustful about his thoughts, Max told himself; what he felt was a steadily growing curiosity and amusement. She was both different from the type of woman Max had always favored and too young for him.

The whole scene was so outrageous that Max threw back his head and laughed aloud. Here he was, in the middle of nowhere, in the grandest house he had ever seen and was ever likely to see, sharing it with a woman who was indisputably a flake, a flake wearing baggy pajamas, painted hair, dirty feet, and a gold snake belt that was probably worth more than his entire wardrobe, a flake who had steaks flown up from Manhattan and a stereo system that rivaled his own stuck in an upstairs room of a house she visited only occasionally.

Maybe, he thought as his laughter subsided into mere chuckles, he was going to have his adventure this summer after all—a very different sort of adventure.

Then he sobered up as he remembered his purpose here. He now began to understand why this matter had to be handled with the utmost delicacy. Nothing could have conveyed the enormous wealth and power of the Vandeveldt family as clearly as Singing Waters did.

A part of Max resented all this wealth and wouldn't have minded seeing it brought down a peg or two, but an even stronger part was both awed and respectful. Great wealth alone could not induce those feelings, but a wealth that had survived many generations stretching all the way back to the original Dutch settlers of the Hudson Valley brought with it an aura of invincibility. Even if it had all come down to the punk rocker upstairs.

He drummed his fingers restlessly on the desktop, wondering how much information he could get about the eccentric Otto Vandeveldt from his equally eccentric niece.

CHAPTER TWO

Annelise put her studio into some semblance of order, then returned to her bedroom in the other wing of the house. The first thing she noticed when she caught sight of herself in the mirror was the streak of red in her hair. She hadn't used that particular color since the arrival of her guest, so she assumed it must have been there all the while.

She grinned into the mirror, an expression that gave her finely boned features a decidedly gamin appearance. She looked like an overage punk rocker. Well, maybe not overage, actually. She knew she looked younger than her twenty-eight years. That was one of the curses of being both small and fine-boned.

How very strange that Professor Armstrong hadn't commented on that streak of paint. But then, who knew what Hilde might have told him about her? "She paints, you see, and I'm afraid that she's a bit eccentric." That statement would have been accompanied by a tiny, self-deprecating shrug that said even the Vandeveldts weren't perfect.

She continued to stare at herself in the mirror, seeing what the professor must have seen. What should she do now? She could further the image he already had of her or she could bring him up short and force him to do a quick reversal. Both choices had their appeal. She made her decision, then went off to shower as she thought about her guest and his reason for being here.

Would all those thousands of pages Otto had left reveal him to have been a genius or a fraud? She was hoping for the former, of course, but could not quite dismiss the possibility of the latter. Otto had certainly been a highly intelligent man, but intelligence becomes genius only if directed, and even as a child, Annelise had sensed that Otto lacked direction much of the time.

As she prepared to play hostess to this unlikely professor, Annelise decided that she'd better learn some more about his intentions. Hilde had been characteristically vague on that subject, saying only that Dr. Armstrong was a theoretical physicist and that he had an interest in Otto's work.

But how did he acquire that interest in the first place? As far as she knew, her uncle had never published anything. He had occasionally attended scientific gatherings, but that was all. It seemed rather strange to her that this professor should suddenly show up, claiming an interest in Otto's work. But then the man himself was a bit strange. He certainly refused to fit into the mold she had cast for him.

As she dressed, Annelise's curiosity grew about both the man and his purpose here.

Max very nearly dropped his drink when she appeared in the doorway of the library. At first, he was convinced that there must be another person in the house. Then, as he belatedly struggled to his feet, his attention focused on that swath of white in the woman's hair. The red was completely gone.

Gone too was the punk rocker. Instead, before him now stood the most incredibly striking woman he had ever seen. With that mane of black and white hair brushed back and tamed into a shining fall, her delicate beauty was exposed to his disbelieving stare. The baggy pajamas had been replaced by a slender ivory silk sheath that caressed a body he simply hadn't imagined before. It took quite a while, however, for him to notice that her feet were still bare, although they appeared to be clean this time, and one slender ankle was encircled by a thin gold chain that shone with tiny diamonds.

He was busy revising his earlier estimate of her age when she

26

advanced into the room, laughing throatily, and gliding across the thick carpet in a way that sent the silk into ripples of unbearable sensuality.

"I guess I forgot to mention that at Singing Waters sitdown dinner means black tie, but since there are no other guests, I'll forgive you this time." Annelise very deliberately fixed her gaze on his jeans-clad form, returning his stare measure for measure.

Max said nothing as he continued to watch that supple body walk gracefully to the bar. He knew that she was fully aware of his shock and probably enjoying it to the hilt, but he just couldn't control it.

"How old are you?" he blurted out finally.

She had unstoppered the decanter of Scotch, and, smiling politely, she paused to turn to him. "Twenty-eight, Professor."

Annelise hated to admit it, but she was feeling almost ashamed of herself. There was a touching honesty to this man. He wasn't even trying to hide his shock by playing the typical "I can handle anything" male role.

"I'll do the steaks and you may prepare the salad," she said and, without asking his preference, poured them each a jigger of Scotch. "Having only recently rediscovered my taste for red meat, I've become very particular about its preparation."

As she sipped at her Scotch, she gave him a level look. "In short, Professor Armstrong, you are an unknown quantity and won't get the chance to screw up. You *can* manage the salad, can't you?"

A grin spread slowly over Max's face as he stared at her. He hadn't any idea which was real—the imperious, high-born lady or the punk rocker.

"I assure you that I'll do my best," he replied dryly, thinking that he'd never met a woman who drank Scotch neat, either. "Have you decided that black and white alone is more suitable to evening wear? The red is gone."

Annelise smiled with pleasure. The professor actually had a sense of humor. What a wonderful discovery. She ran her fingers through her hair. "All sorts of colors have been known to appear in my hair—and on my hands and feet and everywhere else. When I paint in the nude, I can end up looking like a living palette."

She watched him, her expression completely deadpan to see the effect of that statement, then went on.

"Of course, I won't be doing that while you're here. Aunt Hilde would be even more scandalized than she already is."

"Please don't let my presence inhibit you," Max protested with mock seriousness. "What Hilde doesn't know can't hurt anyone. I know how important it is to be, ah, comfortable while you work."

"Thank you," she replied, imitating his dry tone, but unable to keep the twinkle out of her blue eyes. Max Armstrong was definitely moving up a few notches in her estimation.

She started the gas grill on the terrace and then they strolled, drinks in hand, down the grassy slope to the lake. Annelise remained silent as she wrestled with the discovery that she actually liked this man. There'd been no doubting his physical attractiveness, even if he was too big—but now, to her amazement, she was finding other things she liked about him, too.

This unforeseen state of affairs bothered her. She'd been fully prepared to tweak the professor's stuffiness at every possible opportunity, while not in any way permitting him to disturb her work here. But there didn't appear to be any stuffiness to tweak, and it seemed more and more likely that he could interfere with her work. Furthermore, it just wasn't like her to feel such a quick and strong rush of interest in a man.

Max was silent, too, as he made the mental adjustments from thinking of her as a flaky kid to accepting her as a highly desirable woman. Heaven help him, he was even beginning to like that white patch in her hair—which probably meant that it would be gone by tomorrow. If he'd learned nothing else since his arrival at Singing Waters, he'd learned that Annelise Vandeveldt was composed of quicksilver.

28

"The lake temperature is only about fifty degrees right now, so unless you're accustomed to icy swims, you might want to use a wetsuit. There are some at the house and one of them will probably fit you." She felt it wise to keep things completely on a host-guest basis.

"Don't you use one?" he asked, since her tone had seemed to imply that she didn't.

"No, I'm used to it. I've been swimming in the lake all my life. The trick is to make it out to the raft before the cold penetrates, then lie there in the sun and warm up before swimming back. We've all learned to become speed swimmers. And by the way, there are two boats in the boathouse—a rowboat and a small sailboat. The larger sailboat is in Plattsburgh for repairs, and we've never had power boats here, thank God."

They had stopped by the side of the lake. The silence about them was total. Not even a ripple stirred the surface of the water.

"Doesn't it bother you to be here alone?" he asked as he glanced down at the small, frail-looking woman beside him.

She gave him a surprised look. "No, of course not. I feel safer here alone than I do in Manhattan with neighbors close by. Besides, George and Mary are here most of the time."

Her reaction made Max feel rather foolish. Dressed as she was tonight, she seemed so very fragile, and yet, beneath all that silken slenderness, he sensed one very tough and independent woman. He wondered if he would ever stop getting mixed signals from her.

He turned to stare back at the house looming over them. "How old is the house?"

She glanced back at it fondly. "It was completed in 1877, after nearly five years of construction. In those days, it was a four-day trip up here by water and coach, so the family came for the entire summer, together with servants and guests. If you're truly interested, I'll show you an album put together by one of my ancestors, showing its construction and early years."

"1877," he echoed. "Surely it must have at least one ghost."

Annelise shook her head. Guests often raised that possibility. She'd even brought a psychic here once to check it out, much to the family's dismay.

"I'm afraid not. Ghosts only inhabit houses where there was madness or violence of some sort, you see—and my family was and is disgustingly straight."

"Even Uncle Otto?" he asked casually.

Something stirred briefly in Annelise, the minor ripple of an almost-forgotten memory. "Otto might have been slightly bent, rather than perfectly straight. But he was far from mad . . . or violent."

Was it his imagination, or had he heard something in that very slight pause? Max wasn't sure, and she went on, talking about sailing and hiking with her uncle.

"You must have been very close to him, then," Max commented when she had finished.

She nodded. "In some important ways, he was more of a father to me than my own ever was. Otto never married, and Father didn't care much for small children—or even for older ones who had no interest in finance. Otto and I were the family misfits, you see, and that alone would have made us close."

Annelise was glad for this turn in the conversation, and decided to seize the opportunity to tell Max a few truths. She whirled about to face him, catching him by surprise.

"I must be frank, Professor Armstrong. If you unearth proof that my uncle was a fraud, I intend to see that it remains our secret."

Max was shocked by her words and her vehemence, but he tried to hide that from her. "Do you think your uncle was a fraud?"

She shrugged and turned away from him again. "I haven't the foggiest, but there's been some suspicion in the family that he might have been."

"Have you ever looked at his papers?" Max inquired as he

began to consider the problems associated with her fierce protectiveness toward her late uncle.

"Only a bit when I packed them away. Theoretical physics is not one of my favorite subjects. In fact, one might go so far as to say that I'm not even sure what the term means."

Max laughed. "You have a lot of company there, I'm afraid. It just means that we're the ones who scratch our heads and dream up the ideas that others then turn into practical solutions to problems."

"That sounds like Otto," she said with a smile. "He always reminded me a bit of Albert Einstein. In fact, he even looked a little like him toward the end, when his hair had turned white and he'd grown a mustache.

"He left tons and tons of papers. I'm afraid that you don't know what you're in for. They're also very disorderly, since I didn't know what I was packing. Do you read German, by the way?"

"German?" he asked. "I can read it, but I don't speak it well. Why?"

"Some of Otto's notes are in German. You see, he preferred the German side of our family to the Dutch, because he considered the Dutch to be money-grubbers. I guess he kept up his German in part by using it in his notes."

"Do you speak either language?"

"Some German. Also French and a little Gaelic."

"Gaelic?" he queried in surprise.

"My mother is Irish-American and has some relatives in Ireland whom I visit regularly. I like being half Irish. It seems so much less stodgy than being one hundred percent Wasp. So I actually studied Gaelic for a little while even though hardly anybody in Ireland speaks it anymore. I'm surprised that Hilde didn't explain away my eccentricities as resulting from that dark Gaelic strain."

"So that's where the black hair comes from," Max mused. "I was wondering about that."

"Mother's family is also the source of this," Annelise said, running her fingers through the streak of white hair.

There was a brief pause before he stammered, "You . . . you mean that's real—not dyed?"

Annelise laughed merrily. Oh, she'd managed to insert that at just the right moment. The poor professor's head must be spinning now.

She ran her fingers slowly through her hair again—to heighten the drama. "It's like a birthmark. It grew in this way from the beginning. Mother has it and so do several other members of her family."

Max grinned. Now he knew for certain that he liked it. "I'm surprised that you haven't dyed it to match the rest of your hair."

"Oh, I'd never do that. I like it. As I said, I like to identify with my mother's family."

"Rather than the Vandeveldts," he finished for her.

"Exactly," she said. "But since I haven't changed my name, you could say that I'm not denying them completely. What kind of family do you come from, Professor?"

He told her that his family was strictly blue-collar, English on one side and German on the other. He also said that he wished she'd call him "Max." She told him that she really didn't much care for the name "Max," but if that was all he had to offer, she supposed it would have to do.

They began to walk back toward the house, talking about their respective families. Max looked down at the sleek head that barely reached his shoulder and felt some very familiar stirrings. He wondered if he could be falling under a spell. Perhaps Singing Waters didn't have any ghosts, but it might well have a witch.

"There," said Annelise with a dramatic, sweeping gesture, "is the life's work of Uncle Otto."

Max furrowed his brow in dismay. It was even worse than he had feared. There were probably twenty-five or thirty boxes—completely disorganized, according to Annelise. And then there was the additional problem of Otto's language practice. Max hadn't exactly lied when he'd said he could read German, but he was pretty rusty.

He watched his hostess as she squatted down before the boxes in the cavernous attic. That streak of white hair gleamed brightly in the light of a bare overhead bulb and contrasted sharply with the shining ebony curtain that fell forward to obscure her face. Max thought that that unusual hair said it all: Annelise Vandeveldt was composed entirely of contrasts.

She was dressed very conventionally today, though, in jeans and a black lightweight sweater that clung to every curve.

The prospect of being here longer than he'd anticipated didn't bother him as much as he might have expected—until he recalled her impassioned defense of her uncle.

Forget about it, he counseled himself. This one just isn't in the cards. She could end up hating you if the worst turns out to be true. Besides, there was the matter of her wealth. At the moment, Max did not care to examine his feelings about that.

"Those three boxes in the back next to the painting have no papers in them, just personal things like his pipe collection and so forth."

"What's the painting?" he asked. Walking over to lift the dust cover he wondered if his interest in her was actually awakening an interest in art.

She made a face. "Oh, it's an early work by an as-yet-undiscovered great artist."

Then she laughed as he turned to her questioningly. "I presented that to Otto on his birthday when I was thirteen. As you can probably guess from the subject, that was at the height of the Vietnam controversy."

Max nodded as he examined the painting. It was the first work of hers that he could understand: glistening white doves against a dark and turbulent background in which could be seen broken bits of the then-ubiquitous peace symbol.

"It's very good," he said, and meant it.

33

"Otto thought so too. He really liked it, and he was never all that fond of art. It hung in the master bedroom until his death. You see, he and I were the only ones in the family who were opposed to the Vietnam War—or to *any* war, for that matter. I painted it for a dual purpose—to please him and to rattle the chains of the rest of the family."

"Why is it up here now?" Max asked idly as he conjured up an image of her at thirteen.

She frowned at it. "He bequeathed it back to me in his will. I guess I should have taken it with me, but at the time I packed his things shortly after his death, I just couldn't face any reminders of him. I really should do something with it, I suppose."

She had leaned forward to examine it more closely, and Max could hear a wistfulness in her voice. It was becoming disturbingly apparent that the bonds between uncle and niece had indeed been powerful. He looked regretfully at the boxes, then back to her.

She was still staring at the painting and seemed totally unaware of his presence as she hunkered down on her heels and wrapped her arms about her knees. Max felt a nearly overwhelming urge to take her into his arms and comfort her. It was the first indication he'd yet seen of vulnerability in this endlessly fascinating woman.

But even now, in her pensive stillness, she radiated a kind of power he'd never encountered before, a force of personality that he suspected had put off more than one man. He thought about her laments over the trials of being a Vandeveldt and wondered if those difficulties might not have less to do with her family than with the unique nature of her personality.

Then, in a way he would soon learn was characteristic of her, she abruptly broke the spell as she rose to her feet.

"You're going to need some help with the boxes. Let me see if Robbie's around. He's the local boy who helps with the outside work. I heard the mower earlier, so he must be here somewhere."

Max watched as she crossed the floor to one of the dormer windows, pulled it open, and leaned out. He smiled as she presented him with a very pleasing view of a shapely bottom and found it was not easy to force his mind back from fantasyland.

But in an instant those fantasies were abruptly shattered by a high, piercing whistle—the kind some people can make by inserting their fingers into their mouths. He saw her beckon to someone outside, then withdraw and close the window again.

"He'll be up in a minute," she said casually as she brushed some dust from her sleeve.

"Did you make that noise?" he asked incredulously.

She laughed in a way that seemed to affect her entire body. "I surely did, Professor. Otto taught me how to do that. It's the only way to get someone's attention in a place this big."

Max shook his head and chuckled ruefully. "What other surprises do you have in store for me, Annelise?"

She simply smiled, and her eyes twinkled.

"You're not at all what I'd expected," he said, aware of an embarrassing huskiness in his voice.

"Neither are you, Professor Maximilian Armstrong," she responded, and grinned to mask her own discomfort. She was very much aware of the suddenly charged atmosphere between them.

The sound of footsteps below broke the spell and startled them both. When the boy appeared, Annelise introduced them and quickly left them to their task.

As soon as she entered her studio, Annelise knew she wouldn't be able to work now. The light was fine, but her mood definitely wasn't. So she decided to go for a walk to clear her head for her day's work.

But thoughts of Max Armstrong followed her right out of the house and onto the path that wound around the end of the lake into the forest. That man was just far too attractive for her peace of mind, and he was growing more so with every minute, it seemed.

Besides his undeniable physical appeal, he had other qualities she found very intriguing. He was utterly without pretensions, insofar as she could see. Then there was that wonderfully dry sense of humor. Possessed of a lively—if occasionally scathing—wit herself, Annelise cherished that trait in others.

There was something else, too—a calm steadiness of nature. She didn't understand why she should find that quality so very appealing, since it seemed to her that it was only a half-step away from dullness. But there it was.

Yes, Max Armstrong was the most interesting man she'd met in a very long time—even if he was a professor. Annelise had very firm opinions on the subject of academics—as she did on nearly everything else. Besides Hilde, two of her cousins were married to academic dullards, and one of her close friends was about to marry an owlish professor of philosophy. A fate worse than death, in her considered opinion: dreary faculty gatherings and stuffy, closed little cliques. Hilde had managed to persuade her to attend a few such affairs, and only fears of her aunt's wrath had kept Annelise from doing something outrageous during them to relieve her boredom.

She stopped abruptly as a thought struck her. Hilde had made numerous attempts to marry her off to various academics. What if Max was her latest attempt? She still hadn't found out the reason for his interest in Otto's work because she'd been too busy eliciting more personal information.

Was Hilde engaged in a renewed effort to find her a suitable husband? And if her aunt was scheming again, was Max a party to it, or merely an unwitting ally?

Annelise began to conjure up a likely scenario. Hilde had been fond of Otto, though despairing of his eccentricities. She might very well want to see Otto's work receive some credit; in fact, Annelise now recalled that Hilde had argued in favor of hiring someone to go through the papers.

So Hilde meets Max at some faculty affair and decides to kill two birds with one stone. Max has the expertise to deal with Otto's papers, and Max also just happens to be an excellent candidate for husband to her troublesome, still-unmarried niece. To make matters even more convenient, Otto's will had stipulated that the papers must remain at Singing Waters, where, it just so happens, the aforementioned niece is spending the summer—alone.

Annelise smiled. She had to admire her aunt's latest scheme. Obviously, she'd underestimated the woman.

That left only the question of whether or not Max had been a part of this. Her instincts told her that he too was an unwitting pawn, but she couldn't be sure.

Hilde certainly would not be above dropping a few hints to the effect that Vandeveldt largess would be bestowed upon any institution that found Otto's papers to be of interest. In fact, there wouldn't even be a need to drop hints to that effect. The Vandeveldt name alone was sufficient to conjure up images of new laboratories and research projects.

Then there was the fact that Max was in his mid-thirties, an age where one might assume the possibility of marriage had occurred to him. He had expensive hobbies. It might not have escaped Max's attention that Rowan, Hilde's husband, enjoyed a very pleasant life-style, thanks to his wife's fortune.

Once again, Annelise found herself caught in the dilemma that had haunted her all her adult life. She disdained the company of most members of her own class, to whom her money was unimportant, and yet she found herself constantly suspicious whenever she ventured outside that circle.

As she thought about all this, she continued to wander through the forest, leaving behind the path on which she had originally set out. But she knew exactly where she was. For most of her life, she had been wandering these woods, and she knew all the landmarks others might miss: a lightning-blasted tree, a marshy spot, the place where especially large ferns grew. Otto had taught her years ago how to look for such things.

She'd been gone for nearly two hours when she scrambled down the last hill and came again to the path that circled the end of the lake. As she started back toward the house, she spotted Max standing on the dock.

He must have caught sight of her through the trees, because by the time she emerged onto the lawn, he was waiting for her.

"Where were you?" he asked in a voice that was slightly harsh with concern. "I've been looking for you."

"Why?" she asked, wondering what on earth could have happened during her absence.

"Because I couldn't find you," he replied, now seeming more distracted than worried.

She nodded with mock solemnity. "That makes sense, I suppose. You were looking for me because you couldn't find me."

He gave her a rather sheepish grin. "I meant that I was worried when I couldn't find you. It's not a good idea to go off into the woods alone."

She had begun to walk toward the house, but now she turned around and gave him a calculatedly surprised look. "My dear professor, I've been walking alone in these woods for years."

"Then someone should have told you that it might be dangerous."

"I'll take your opinion under advisement," she rejoined dryly. "Does that also apply to you? I was under the impression that you intend to take that ugly motorcycle of yours out into the woods."

"I'm used to the woods," he said defensively.

"Not to *these* woods, you're not—but *I* am."

"I picked up some maps of the region," he continued. "And I always carry a compass and a handgun."

"I carry my instincts," she replied smugly.

"I still think it's dangerous for you to be out there alone, Annelise," he persisted, though with less certainty.

"And I think you're showing some definite signs of incipient male chauvinism, Professor."

Max said nothing because he knew she was right. He didn't understand why he'd overreacted to her disappearance, because this was one female who didn't appear to require male protection from anything.

Annelise saw his confusion and pounced on it. "If we're to

survive living in the same house, it might be wise to lay down a few ground rules right now. And rule number one is that I am answerable to no one for my time and actions. You are free to do as you please, and I will certainly do as *I* please."

"I imagine you always have," Max responded in an amused tone. "Do you know how easily you fall into that lady-of-the-manor tone at times?"

She did, and didn't care to learn that it had no effect whatsoever upon him, other than amusement. "Let's not turn this into a discussion on elitism," she said sharply.

Max just continued to smile at her. "I think it's a defense mechanism."

"And I think you are rapidly becoming a pain in the neck," she stated angrily, then marched off toward the rear of the house.

Max watched her stalk away and cursed himself for a fool. She'd made him sound like some sort of macho idiot, so he'd responded in kind. If only she'd settle down into being one person, perhaps he could gain some control over himself. She'd had him off balance since the moment he'd arrived at Singing Waters, and Max was totally unaccustomed to such a state of affairs.

More than a little apprehensive, Max had seen numerous men who had gotten themselves mixed up with the wrong kind of woman, but no such thing had ever happened to him. He'd always applied the same cool-headed logic to his love affairs that he did to his work, and with equally satisfactory results.

But if there was ever a wrong woman and a wrong time, it was this woman and this time. And yet, she fascinated him and brought to his life an excitement he'd rarely known.

He started back to the house, too, reminding himself that he had a purpose here, one that did not include falling for the mistress of Singing Waters.

Annelise stormed into the kitchen, where she paused only long enough to grab a container of yogurt before stomping her way up the back stairs to her studio. Those final words she'd flung at him followed along after her. They had been calculated to shock, and she guessed from his reaction that they'd accomplished that purpose. She sank onto the floor of her studio and ate the yogurt while she thought about Max Armstrong.

Okay, so he'd overreacted to her disappearance. There wasn't anything so unusual about that, really. Because of her diminutive size, men often thought of her as frail and helpless. However, that impression was generally dispelled after about five minutes of conversation. Somehow, the professor just hadn't gotten the message yet.

Still, he'd done nothing to justify her scathing remark—except, of course, for seeing through her feigned haughtiness. She'd always used that gambit very successfully in the past. Men were invariably chastised when she used what he had called her lady-of-the-manor tone. Max, however, had merely found it amusing.

She frowned. Annelise certainly wasn't about to admit—even to herself—that things might be moving out of her control, but the fact that she could even be considering that possibility was disturbing. Annelise Vandeveldt had been in control of herself and those around her for most of her life. No matter how much she might criticize her family, they had generally done just what she wanted them to do. And the men who had passed through her life had done so completely on her terms.

Downstairs, the object of her thoughts had begun to delve into Otto's papers. His hope of finding some order among the boxes had been quickly dashed, as was his hope that the papers would be dated. Whatever filing system the man had employed had been totally destroyed by Annelise's packing—if it had ever existed in the first place.

Accustomed to the orderliness of the scientific mind, Max was aghast at the apparent randomness of Otto Vandeveldt's work. Even his initial, cursory examination revealed that the man jumped from one line of thought to another. But despite this, Max found himself becoming interested in Otto's ideas. Whatever else he might prove to have been, Otto Vandeveldt had certainly been an original thinker.

It quickly became apparent to Max that Otto would never have survived the structured environment of a university. But given his comfortable circumstances, he had not needed to concern himself with that. A small part of Max began almost unconsciously to envy Otto the wealth that had given him such freedom.

Immersing himself in his work had had the beneficial effect of taking his mind off his hostess, but when the throbbing bass of her stereo penetrated even the thick walls of the house, Max found his thoughts returning to her again. He considered going upstairs to ask her to turn it down, but decided against it when he realized that she might be waiting for him to do just that.

Although he had known her for only twenty-four hours, Max suspected that her anger was probably as impermanent as the rest of her. He had thought about apologizing, but couldn't see any reason to do so. He might have been tactless, but he hadn't been wrong. That hauteur of hers was a pose and a defense mechanism, a way of holding the world at bay. If no one had ever pointed that out to her in the past, then the truth was long overdue.

But Max suspected that she knew perfectly well how she had sounded. In fact, he was quite certain that Annelise Vandeveldt knew exactly what she was doing at *all* times. "Strong-willed" was the mildest term he could think of to describe her.

After a few more moments of thinking about her to the accompaniment of that annoying music, he finally managed to tune out both music and his hostess and return to his work.

CHAPTER THREE

There is an ancient sense that can warn people of approaching danger, and those whose professions or hobbies carry them into threatening situations seem able to develop that sense. So it was that even as he was concentrating on Otto's legacy, Max began to feel that little prickle of awareness that made him look around quickly.

She was standing in the open doorway to the library. Max had no idea how long she'd been there, but something told him that she hadn't just arrived. For just a moment, she seemed almost nervous, but then that fleeting impression vanished as she folded her arms across her chest and smiled.

"One problem with being a Vandeveldt is that we never apologize, because that would mean admitting to imperfections we couldn't possibly have. However, sometimes we very graciously try to make amends. How do you feel about Whoppers with cheese and onion rings?"

Max's grin grew until he was laughing heartily, and Annelise finally relaxed. She'd been counting on his sense of humor and was happy to see that she'd been right.

"Are you telling me that's all the town has to offer?" he asked when he had stopped laughing. "Or is it just that you don't feel the offense warrants a more serious making of amends?"

"The former, I'm afraid. The town's only restaurant is closed temporarily because of a very messy divorce. One can only hope that he will find a new business manager or she will find a new chef. Regular bulletins are issued by Mrs. M., and at last report, it was still closed."

She advanced into the room, looking at the boxes surrounding Max. "So, is it worse than you'd expected?"

"I'm afraid so," he admitted ruefully. "If Otto had a filing system at all, it didn't survive the packing."

"Oh, he had a system, all right. I believe it consisted of filling one drawer after another in an order known only to him. You see, he had several filing cabinets in here, in addition to the drawers in the desk and the built-in drawers below the bookshelves."

Max chuckled. "You were right about his lack of discipline— from what I've seen so far, anyway. But he *was* brilliant; I have no doubt of that."

Annelise smiled. "And he was happy, too, because he was doing just what he wanted to do."

She sank down onto the floor across from him. "How did you come to be interested in his work? As far as I know, he'd never published anything. Did Hilde or Rowan mention him?"

"Rowan had mentioned him, but only in a general way. My interest in Otto's work came about through a man named Robert Harrington, who was once on the MIT faculty."

"I don't recognize the name," she replied, shrugging.

"I don't suppose you would. I never met him, either. He disappeared twenty years ago," he said carefully.

"Disappeared?"

Max nodded. "He was a theoretical physicist, too, and he must have met Otto at some scientific gathering. They apparently corresponded regularly and met fairly frequently. Then Harrington just vanished.

"He wasn't married and lived alone. After some period of time, his relatives had him declared legally dead. The school got the papers that had been in his office, and a relative moved into his house. She died recently, and when the house was being cleared out to be sold, someone found more papers that had been stored in the attic all these years.

"So they contacted us and my department head turned them over to me because my present field of interest happens to coincide with the work that was discovered. In them, I found references to Otto and his work. Since I knew Rowan and Hilde, I asked them for permission to look at Otto's work, too."

Annelise had to work hard not to let her relief show. Her worst fears had been proved groundless, after all. Of course, she had no doubt that Hilde had fairly leapt at the idea, but still, it was all perfectly innocent.

"But I don't see how work done twenty years ago could have any importance today, and Otto died over five years ago himself. Surely your field has advanced far beyond any work either of them might have done."

"Physics is an incredibly broad field, Annelise. There are even theories of Einstein's from back in the thirties that have never been fully explored. Only in the past year or so have I turned my attention to areas those two were exploring back then. And it's possible that they might have gotten further than I have."

Annelise smiled with pleasure. "It would be so wonderful if Otto turned out to have made a real contribution to science. If that happens, I think I'd be tempted to go visit my father's grave just to say, 'I told you so.'"

Then she grimaced. "What an awful thing to say. I should send myself upstairs to wash out my mouth with soap."

Max laughed. "I suspect that might have happened a few times."

"Oh, it did. I was always at my worst up here because I had to compete with my older cousins. I was the despair of the entire family—except for Otto, of course. He almost always defended me. His favorite phrase was, 'Let little Nellie be herself.' Unfortunately, the others didn't agree with him."

"But I'm sure you managed anyway—to be yourself, I mean."

"Of course. Not even my family is a match for me when I put my mind to it. What did Hilde tell you about me?"

"Very little. She said that you were an artist, and that's about

44

all—although I did get the impression that she disapproved of something."

"She disapproves of *everything*, where I'm concerned. And what she probably said was that I 'painted.' Hilde does not consider me to be an artist. Furthermore, she won't rest until she has me married off like all my cousins."

"They're all married?" Max asked, thinking again about that niece he was supposed to have met at the dinner party.

"Yes, all of them—and to 'suitable' spouses, too. So you can see that she's becoming rather desperate. Heaven only knows what I might bring into the family if I'm not given some guidance."

"Have you ever come close to that—marrying, I mean?"

"Not at all. However, just to ruffle their feathers, I *have* brought friends to family gatherings from time to time. I have some very interesting friends," she finished with an impish grin.

Max didn't doubt that at all, and he felt strangely relieved that she'd never come close to marriage, not that any man could capture this will-o'-the-wisp. Ahh, he thought, but the challenge . . . !

"I think you offered to buy me a gourmet dinner. After yogurt for lunch, I might even want *two* Whoppers."

"Well, I don't know about that, Professor. There are limits to my generosity."

As they were walking toward the garage, Annelise suggested that they take her car. Max consented, although he had some reservations. He'd already admired her sleek, gray Porsche and wouldn't have minded driving it himself, but he doubted that was what she had in mind.

It seemed unlikely that she could be a good driver, given her erratic nature, and Max was thinking uneasily about the winding mountain road between Singing Waters and the village. Still, he was reluctant to suggest that he drive, because he sensed that despite their rapprochement, something was still troubling her. He reflected with some amusement that he'd never before encountered anyone who could draw an invisible line about herself and post a "Keep Out" sign quite as effectively as she did, while somehow managing to maintain a façade of friendliness.

Well, he thought, whatever's bothering her, I'm bound to find out soon. If there was one thing he could say with reasonable certainty about this unpredictable woman, it was that she wouldn't hide her feelings for very long.

Max admired the car and the sound of the powerful engine as she started it, then thought about her so-called rebellion against her family. It was a safe bet that she hadn't acquired the Porsche from her earnings as an artist.

Then, as she backed the car out of the garage, he realized that he didn't really know whether or not she was a successful artist. Hilde had, as Annelise had guessed, dismissed her niece's painting as being nothing more than a pastime, and after meeting Annelise, Max had been inclined to accept that judgment. It seemed to him that art, like any other profession, must require self-discipline; and Annelise, like the uncle she had adored, did not strike him as being a highly disciplined person.

"Are you good?" he asked, following his thoughts without considering the strangeness of the question.

She threw him an amused glance as she shifted gears. "You mean as a driver?"

"No," he answered quickly as he realized that she must have guessed his uneasiness about that. "I meant as an artist."

"Oh, I'm good, but I'm not yet into greatness—and maybe I never will be, either," she added with a trace of uncertainty that surprised him. However, she recovered quickly and continued in a brisk tone.

"I have a one-woman show in September at a prominent Manhattan gallery, and I think that I've earned it on the basis of my work alone and not on my family's name."

Max wondered if he should be taking her complaints about the trials of being a Vandeveldt more seriously. Still, it was almost impossible to apply the phrase "poor little rich girl" to this totally self-possessed woman. Surely he'd just imagined that hint of uncertainty a moment ago.

"I don't know anything at all about art," he admitted. "I've bought a few paintings, but only because I liked them and not because I can really appreciate them."

"No one should ever buy art for any other reason, Max. My father, for example, bought for investment, without any interest at all in the works themselves."

"You really disliked your father, didn't you?" Max asked curiously.

She shifted gears again with commendable expertise, then smiled briefly. "One does not dislike one's parents. Let's just say that we disappointed each other. Otto and I fell into the same category as far as Father was concerned. If we hadn't been blood relatives, he would have been happy to have ignored us altogether. My brother, however, would tell you that he was a wonderful, brilliant man."

"Tell me about your brother," Max urged, feeling almost embarrassingly curious about her family. America might not have royalty, but with families like the Vandeveldts, it came very close.

"There isn't much to tell. He's two years older than I am and gives every indication of following in Father's footsteps. Except in his choice of a wife, that is. Father at least had the good sense to choose Mum, but Chris has this pale nothing of a wife: good family, good breeding, no brains and no ambition other than to appear on everyone's list of prominent socialites. She was a classmate of mine at the school where we were both sent to be properly 'finished.' She was and I wasn't."

Max laughed. "I don't think you ever will be, either."

"Will be what?" she asked, glancing at him again.

"Finished. There are far too many of you for it ever to come together as a single, finished product."

She didn't respond, and he glanced at her, hoping that he hadn't insulted her.

"I think I like that." She nodded and smiled, turning to him briefly. "Thank you—even if it wasn't intended as a compliment."

"It was," he assured her. Everything about Annelise spelled excitement to Max. Sitting here now beside her, he had that same adrenaline-charged high he always felt at the beginning of a climb or a caving expedition, and he also had that same deepdown feeling of danger.

His concern about her driving skills evaporated quickly as they reached the main road and she put the car through its paces effortlessly. She sailed through the curves with the skill of a Grand Prix racer, all the while keeping up a casual conversation. Max was both impressed and disconcerted.

He continued to think about the challenge she represented. No woman had ever truly challenged him this way before. Mountains, raging rivers, uncharted caves—all these were challenges. Exploring the frontiers of physics was another sort of challenge. But for Max women had always been there for the taking.

Blessed with the rugged good looks that most women seemed to prefer, and then further blessed with an easygoing, wryly humorous nature, Max had never had trouble attracting women. But he knew that attracting this particular woman could be a very great challenge. For the moment, he preferred not to consider the wisdom of accepting that challenge.

They reached their destination, got their meals, and took them to one of the outside tables, where Annelise proceeded to perch cross-legged on one of the benches and devour her onion rings and burger with gusto.

Max watched her bite into her Whopper and decided that perhaps the most delightful thing about her was that unique zest for life that she seemed to bring to everything.

Although she seemed totally unaware of it, Max noticed the attention they were receiving from other customers. It was understandable, of course. This was a small town and there couldn't be anything else in or near it comparable to the Vandeveldts. On the other hand, no matter who she was, Annelise would have attracted attention. He doubted that she went unnoticed even in places where people had never heard the name Vandeveldt.

"Well," she said suddenly, giving him an impish grin, a dab of ketchup in one corner of her mouth, "I think the Darnells have just been replaced as the hot gossip item around town."

Max really hadn't intended to do it, but his hand just picked itself up and reached out to wipe away that spot of ketchup before he could stop it. They stared at each other in silence for an instant before he withdrew his hand self-consciously and cleaned it with his napkin. Then he asked her what she meant.

"Oh, the Darnells are the couple who have the restaurant and are in the midst of a very messy divorce. But now everyone will forget about them and start whispering about the notorious Annelise Vandeveldt, who is conducting an affair up at the house."

She hurried through her explanation with a self-consciousness of her own. It would have been amusing a moment ago, before he had touched her like that. How very strange that both of them seemed to think that such a gesture was in some way intimate. She raised a finger to touch the spot he had touched.

"I see," Max said as he watched her reaction with considerable satisfaction. "Has the 'notorious' Annelise Vandeveldt done this sort of thing before?"

"No, she hasn't, and she isn't going to this time, either," she stated with unnecessary firmness.

Max said nothing at all, which only served to keep her words hanging there between them, becoming ever more embarrassing.

"I didn't mean to insult you, Max. I'm glad you're here," Annelise finally said. Then she decided that that hadn't been the right thing to say, either. She didn't know him well enough to be encouraging him. Her whole life had been built around discouraging men while she took her time deciding what to do about them.

"I'm glad I am, too," Max said and smiled. At the moment, not even Alpine peaks could have lured him away.

They munched away in silence for a few minutes, and then she announced that she had to have another order of onion rings.

Annelise got up to get them before he could offer to do it for her, and he watched her make her way past the other tables. She moved with all the grace and self-possession of a small, sleek cat and was followed by every eye in the place.

Max thought about men who deliberately went for highly visible women as a way of bolstering their own egos. He couldn't think of any woman he'd ever dated who could have been considered a real head-turner. Beauty just hadn't been at the top of his list. But he couldn't deny a certain rather smug satisfaction at being seen with her, and that bothered him. He was still contemplating it when she returned.

"Why haven't you married, Max?" she asked as soon as she'd seated herself.

Her words, like everything else about her, caught him off guard. He really should be getting used to this by now, he thought as he wondered what had prompted this question.

"I guess it's because I haven't found the right woman yet," he said and shrugged.

"Have you been looking—seriously, I mean?"

"No, I can't really say that I've been looking seriously," he answered honestly, still at a loss to explain why they were discussing this particular topic.

"Well, I should think it's about time you did—and preferably for someone rich enough to keep you in style while you pursue your academic career."

Now he knew exactly where this conversation was headed. Her challenge was unmistakable. His tone was casual and very slightly amused as he answered her.

"I think I can manage to support myself and a family if it came to that. Academic salaries at good schools aren't that bad these days."

His reaction irritated her because it wasn't at all what she'd expected. So she goaded him some more. "I've always heard that it's fairly common practice for scholars to find themselves rich wives. Uncle Rowan is a perfect example."

"Rowan Newcombe is a highly respected economist," Max pointed out mildly.

"Of course he is. I didn't mean to imply otherwise. And I happen to know that he loves Aunt Hilde very much, although I can't imagine why. But you must admit that her money does grease life's little bumps for him. If he didn't have her, he'd be forced to spend his summers out money-grubbing in industry, instead of sailing and traveling."

"Only if he happened to place a high premium on luxuries," Max replied in the same mild tone.

"Do *you* place a high premium on them, Max?" she asked, looking at him intently.

"I'm here—not out money-grubbing, as you put it. And I've already told you how I usually spend my summers."

She continued to stare at him for a few more seconds; then, as her gaze slid away, her expression turned thoughtful. "Hmm, that's true. But those hobbies of yours must be expensive, and if you had to support a family, you'd probably be forced to give them up."

"Very few men are the sole support of their families anymore," Max pointed out, taking care to keep from smiling. "And if I married, I'd probably have to give up most of it anyway—unless my wife wanted to join me."

After a long silence, she gave him a somewhat sheepish look that didn't sit naturally on her face. "You'll have to excuse my skepticism, but over the years, I've learned that even those who have no interest in money suddenly find it fascinating when they come near it."

Max thought briefly about confronting this issue head on, but decided against it—for now. "What you're saying is that you've had men pursue you for your money."

"Exactly."

"And that's why you've decided to be impossible."

She stared at him for a moment, then burst out laughing.

"Max, you've missed your calling. You should have been a psychologist."

Max thought with considerable satisfaction that she seemed just a bit nervous. "Are there any men in your life now?"

"If there were, I wouldn't be up here alone." She paused, then made a dismissive gesture. "No, strike that. Even if there were, I still would have come up here alone. Men and work don't mix."

"I've noticed the same thing about women and work," he observed with a smile.

"Oh?" She asked as a smile curved her mouth, too.

"Nothing personal intended, of course."

"Oh, of course not—for me, either." She resumed her meal quickly.

Max drained the last of his soda as he watched her trying to pay attention to everything but him. He wondered how he was doing on that scorecard she was keeping. His profession hadn't scored very well; he already knew that. But her uncharacteristic nervousness told him that he might be doing well enough otherwise. Even those thinly disguised attempts to rile him served in a perverse way to show her interest.

She finished her meal and began to collect the remnants to put in the trash, still avoiding his gaze. When she got up, there was a certain stiffness to the movement that told him she was very much aware of his scrutiny.

He continued to watch her as she carried the trash to the barrel. What would she be like in bed, he wondered? Would she be as elusive and everchanging there as she seemed to be in every other way? And would he find there that unique combination of boldness and shyness?

Max shook himself mentally. "Try not to lose sight of those problems, old buddy," he muttered to himself.

Annelise was having one of those days when nothing seemed quite right. She didn't want to paint, a walk in the woods seemed inadvisable because of the dark clouds that were gathering, and she didn't think she should interrupt Max at his work.

She glared at the unsatisfactory attempt she'd made to paint, then put her brushes in to soak and sank down in an old leather beanbag chair she kept in the studio. Otto was on her mind today —not surprisingly, since Max had been talking about her uncle's work and asking all sorts of questions about him. She'd enjoyed talking about Otto with someone she believed just might appreciate him.

She gave her memories free rein for a while, recalling that complex man. Max saw him as a brilliant, if undisciplined scientist, but she remembered him as a gentle, kind man, whose behavior toward her had always belied his somewhat stern appearance. Her brother and cousins had always been rather frightened of him, but fear would never have occurred to the indomitable Annelise.

Her overwhelming love for Singing Waters stemmed in large part from having spent her childhood summers there with her uncle. An enthusiastic outdoorsman and conservationist, Otto had abhorred hunting and would never permit a gun to be brought onto the premises—a dictum that was still followed five years after his death.

From him, Annelise had learned the patience required to observe all manner of wild creatures going about their routines. When Otto and she had gone on their treks, he had always carried a bird book and a wildflower guide, and she often carried those same books with her now on her solitary walks.

Alone among his generation of Vandeveldts, Otto had opposed the war in Vietnam and had given freely to peace organizations. He'd also supported both the civil rights and women's movements, provoking heated arguments among his siblings on all those subjects. During most of that time, Annelise herself hadn't really been old enough to understand the arguments completely, but that hadn't prevented her from loudly defending her uncle's views.

She continued to drift with her memories and came again to the one that had surfaced the other day in the attic: Otto's pleasure in that painting she'd done for him. She remembered it well because although he'd always encouraged her in her art, before that painting he'd never shown much interest in the results.

She began to think about the painting, which she'd unimaginatively entitled "Peace." It seemed wrong that she had permitted it to remain hidden away in the attic all these years. By now, she could remember Otto's pleasure in it and forget the pain of associating it with his death.

She frowned. The owner of the gallery that was presenting her show had indicated an interest in another of her early works that hung in her SoHo loft. He'd suggested that using a few of her earlier paintings in the show might be interesting, but she'd ignored the suggestion because there was only that one still in existence. The others she'd destroyed in a fit of disgust some years ago.

Perhaps it might be interesting to exhibit "Peace." It *did* have something, even if that something was only a certain nostalgia. But the generation that could best appreciate that nostalgia was the very same generation from which her potential customers would be drawn. And hadn't she been telling herself that it was time she became a little more commercial about her art? She'd never consider selling the painting, of course. She'd done it expressly for Otto, and he'd bequeathed it back to her. In fact, it had been the only personal item mentioned in his will. The bulk of his estate had been left to a charitable trust, along with a sizable bequest to Annelise and far smaller ones to his other nieces and nephews.

Yes, she thought as she got out of the chair, that painting might be just right for the show. And in any event, it was time to rescue it from the attic.

She went off to the third floor, then climbed the steep, narrow staircase to the attic, lost in thought about the show. If it didn't go well, she might be forced to agree with Hilde that she was just someone who "painted," a rich girl with a pleasant little hobby.

She went over to the painting and removed the dust cover, hoping that the extremes of temperature in the attic hadn't harmed the canvas. A close examination revealed no damage, but she knew she couldn't be sure until she had it downstairs in the bright light of her studio. So Annelise picked it up and started back down the stairs.

Before she had gotten to the bottom of the attic steps, she felt the wood frame begin to loosen. The canvas might have survived the attic intact, but the frame apparently hadn't. Probably the glue in the joints had dried out. Tightening her grip, and holding the bottom braced against herself, she continued slowly down the next flight of stairs.

By the time she finally reached the studio, she was walking bent over in an effort to keep the frame from falling apart entirely. She set it down carefully onto the studio floor, then stepped away to look it over.

Even back then, Annelise had done all her own framing and she'd always used the finest materials, including glue. While the attic was scarcely the best of environments, she was still somewhat surprised that the frame hadn't held together. She bent to examine the side that had pulled apart and frowned when she saw traces of some amber-colored material at the corners. The glue she always used was clear, so that any traces wouldn't show.

Cautiously, she pulled away the broken side, then stopped and stared at it. The wood strip had carried with it a sheet of lined yellow tablet paper. The back of her neck became suddenly cold and prickly as she immediately recognized both the paper and the writing on it. Otto had always used that yellow, legal-sized paper, and there was no mistaking his small, neat handwriting.

She extricated the sheet of paper from the broken frame, losing part of it in the process, then sat back on the floor to read it. But that quickly proved to be impossible. It might as well have been written in Sanskrit for all she understood.

Then Annelise very carefully lifted the canvas away from its backing and discovered just what she'd expected. By the time she had extracted them all from their hiding place, she had nine more pages, all of them equally incomprehensible.

What on earth was going on? Otto might have been eccentric, but he hadn't been crazy enough to have hidden his work. It just didn't make sense.

She spread out the papers and peered at them again, seeking some clue among the scientific gibberish. They were all filled with calculations and symbols, and were probably meaningful only to someone like Max.

She gathered them together and started for the doorway, eager to show them to him. Then, just outside her studio, she stopped. Wasn't she being a bit hasty? Otto must have hidden them for a reason. All his other work had lain open to view; he'd never even locked his filing cabinets.

She chewed her lower lip, torn between her desire to show the papers to Max and a feeling that she should give the matter some thought first. Finally—and uncharacteristically—discretion won out over curiosity and she carried the papers to her bedroom and hid them beneath some sweaters in her dresser drawer. After that, she laughed nervously at her melodramatic behavior.

Annelise looked out the window and saw that the weather had apparently made up its mind in favor of sunshine, so she decided to go for a walk. She always thought better in the solitude of the forest, and she definitely had some serious thinking to do now. So she hurried down the front staircase, then stopped. Since that first day, she'd made a concession to his concern for her safety— something she didn't think he fully appreciated. Whenever she went for a walk, she always let him know.

She stopped at the library doorway when she saw Max sitting on the floor, reading intently. Once again, she thought about bringing the papers to him, but before she could make up her mind, he looked up, and his frown of concentration changed to a welcoming smile. Feeling an odd sense of pleasure, she very nearly blurted out her secret.

"I'm going for a walk," she announced hurriedly, eager to be away before she could give in to that impulse.

Max nodded. He knew that this was a concession on her part and about as much a one as he was likely to get. If she'd invited him to join her, he would have jumped at the chance, but he was reluctant to push. More than anyone he'd ever met, Annelise required space—perhaps too much space to permit him ever to get close to her.

"Enjoy yourself," he said. "But it might be a rainy walk."

"No, the sky is really clearing this time. I'm not going far—just along that path on the other side of the lake."

Then she turned abruptly and left. Why had she done that? Next thing, she'd be drawing him maps. So much for her big speech about being accountable to no one.

She crossed the broad lawn and moved swiftly along the path around the end of the lake. Unlike most of her walks, this one had a specific destination. Ten minutes after leaving the house, she had come to her favorite spot—a small clearing near the far end of the lake where spongy moss grew thickly down to the water's edge and the absence of trees permitted a lovely view of the house. She sat down, inhaling the damp, earthy fragrance she loved.

Damn it, Otto, she cursed silently. Why did you do that? I know you must have had a reason, but what could it be and how could you think I'd understand?

Then she sighed heavily and forced herself to consider the situation logically.

Otto had bequeathed the painting with its secret to her, and he would certainly have known that she'd never sell it. No doubt he'd expected her to take it home with her, which is exactly what she would have done if his sudden death hadn't left her unable to handle any memories of him.

And if she had taken it home, she certainly would have reframed it. She had never liked the frame he had told her to use in the first place, and had told him that, offering to reframe it only a year or so before his death. Furthermore, even if she hadn't reframed it, she would have noticed his inexpert regluing.

So he had deliberately left those papers where she—and no one else—would find them. If he'd simply wanted to guarantee their safekeeping, he could have put them into the safe. But that way, any family member could have found them after his death. And if he'd left them for her only, there would have been questions from the others.

Obviously, Otto had wanted her and her alone to have those papers and hadn't wanted anyone else even to know of their existence.

"Wonderful," she muttered. Perfect logic so far. But it must surely have occurred to Otto that she couldn't possibly know the significance of the papers, let alone what to do with them.

She began to wonder if he might have given her some hint of their existence or meaning at some point. Even during Otto's last years, when she'd been busy with her life in Manhattan, they'd still spent a lot of time together here at Singing Waters. She'd always come up before the others, specifically to have time alone with her uncle, and she'd visited him other times during the year, too.

In the last few years of his life, Otto had become mildly hypertensive, but had responded well to medication and a low-salt diet. Then, in one of those calamities medical science can't explain, he'd suffered a massive stroke that had left him almost totally paralyzed. For two weeks, he'd lain in the hospital, drifting in and out of reality, his speech severely affected by the paralysis.

Annelise had come up to be with him during those final two weeks of his life, and both she and Hilde had been there at the end. During part of that terrible time, he had seemed to know she was there and would talk disjointedly about their times together. Later, she had tried to block that time out of her mind because it hurt too much to remember his twisted face and pitiful attempts to communicate.

The passage of time had dulled the pain somewhat, but Annelise still found tears stinging her eyes as she recalled it now. She forced herself to think about those final weeks, but could recall nothing that might have been an attempt to tell her about the papers.

At first, nothing came to her clearly, but then, as she was about to give up, she *did* recall something. It came back to her because there had seemed to be a note of urgency in his voice at the time. He had reminded her of a discussion they had had years before, one that had had to do with scientific responsibility. He'd told her that many scientists believed they bore no responsibility at all for the use to which their discoveries would be put, and had asked her what she thought, using as his example the men who had created the atomic bomb during World War II.

Annelise had very firmly expressed the opinion that scientists *did* bear responsibility for their inventions. Otto had agreed with her, but had then pointed out the American lives saved by the use of that bomb and the peaceful uses to which atomic energy could be put.

"The dilemma occurs, Nellie, when you've discovered something that could be used for great good or for great evil."

Annelise shuddered as a chill passed through her. The words she'd just recalled had been spoken not by a dying man in a hospital, but by a much healthier one. And they'd been spoken as the two of them had sat in this very spot. It frightened her that they should come back now, years later as though they had somehow been lying in wait here all this time.

At the time, she'd assumed he was talking only in generalities —but now she wondered. Had her gentle, peace-loving uncle discovered a way to build bigger and better bombs? The thought filled her with horror, even though she told herself she was being melodramatic. Would Otto have bequeathed such a dilemma to her?

There was one way to find out—but she wasn't yet ready to take that step.

CHAPTER FOUR

After Annelise had hastily departed, Max tilted back the big desk chair, propped his feet on the desk and stared at the doorway she had so recently occupied. The now empty space seemed to him to still be charged with her presence.

He wondered, as he had so often done during the past few days, what was going on in her mind. Her behavior toward him ran the gamut from somewhat stilted politeness to a rather wary friendliness. He even fancied that on a few occasions, she had shown more than a casual interest in him.

Some men, he supposed, might push their advantage, but Max sensed that that was the worst possible thing he could do. Although he still found it virtually impossible to think of her as being at all shy, she nevertheless reminded him of the deer that came down in the early evening to drink out of the lake. As long as he remained perfectly still, they stayed; but if he made a move, they simply vanished. Max did not want Annelise to vanish.

Yesterday, to his pleasure and surprise, the music that filtered down from her studio had changed abruptly from rock to Rachmaninoff—specifically, the hauntingly beautiful "Rhapsody on a Theme of Paganini." Telling himself that he needed a break anyway, he'd gone up to her studio to comment on the welcome change.

And there she'd been, standing before the same large canvas with her back to him as she worked with a tiny brush. The afternoon had become quite warm, and she was wearing a pair of

61

cutoff denims that had perhaps seen a bit too much of the scissors. She'd already acquired a light tan on her slender legs, but a bit of pale skin peeked out just below the ragged fringe as she bent to her work. Her T-shirt was stretched snugly across her back, and Max immediately noted the absence of a bra strap.

After watching her silently for a few moments, he left without drawing her attention. Then he'd spent the next hour wondering if she really did sometimes paint in the nude. If a heat wave descended upon Singing Waters, or if the music changed to "Bolero," he didn't think he'd be able to stand it.

He got up from the desk, stretched his long frame, and then decided to go have another look at her work. He was trying hard to understand it hoping it would help him to understand *her*, something that was rapidly becoming an obsession.

The first thing he saw when he entered her studio was the painting from the attic, lying on the studio floor with its frame broken. He muttered a curse at the fact that she had apparently been unwilling to ask him to carry it down here for her. It was a miracle that she hadn't broken herself along with the frame.

He bent to examine the painting in the bright light of the studio, but immediately noticed a piece of yellow paper clinging to the broken frame. Curious, Max picked up the strip of wood—and then he too knew a moment of prickly, breathless awareness.

He recognized Otto's small, neat handwriting immediately, and continued to hold his breath as he scanned the lines. Then, his appetite whetted, Max cautiously lifted the canvas away from its backing to see if there was more hidden there. When he found nothing, he swore aloud and looked around the studio.

Something had obviously been hidden in the painting—and Annelise had found it as a result of the broken frame. But where was the rest of it? And why would Otto have hidden his work?

Max read the lines on the paper again. There wasn't much there, but one partial equation on the scrap stood out tantalizingly. It was the first real evidence that Max had yet seen to indicate that Otto might indeed have been engaged in the work he had denied existed after Harrington's disappearance—the work Harrington had claimed he and Otto had been doing.

He abruptly cut off this speculation as he began to wonder why Annelise hadn't brought this discovery to him. She couldn't possibly have understood it.

His elation over this possible discovery suddenly evaporated as he faced the fact that she obviously hadn't trusted him enough to bring this to him. He was startled to realize that her trust was far more important to him than Otto's work.

So now, Max too faced a dilemma. How could he persuade her to trust him—something he wanted in any event—without also ultimately giving her the best of reasons to distrust him?

The warm sun was making very little progress in thawing her chilled body, but Annelise knew that only a part of that chill came from her plunge into the icy waters of the lake.

Max had declined the invitation she'd issued to join her for a swim. Perhaps he'd taken her distraction as an indication of her lack of interest in him. That wasn't the case at all, but Otto's strange "bequest" had managed to push thoughts of Max onto the back burner for the time being.

She could, of course, solve both those problems by taking Max into her confidence, but she had already decided against that. He was too new to her life to be privy to this secret. Intimacy in any form was something Annelise did not grant easily or quickly.

She lay flat on her back on the fiberglass raft, wearing nothing more than a tiny triangle of black cloth. Her bra top had been discarded, as was her habit in the privacy of Singing Waters. Two summers on the Riviera had replaced her American prudishness with European tolerance.

What on earth was she to do about those papers? She didn't *have* to do anything at all, of course. She could just stash them away somewhere and eventually forget about them. Or she could even destroy them. They might well be worthless by now, in any event. It had been eight or nine years since Otto had had that discussion with her about scientific responsibility—and the work itself could be older than that, for all she knew.

But she recalled Max's statement about the broadness of the field of theoretical physics, and his own interest in work that Otto and that MIT professor had done more than twenty years ago. So those hidden papers might indeed still be valuable. But how was she to know, unless she gave them to someone who could understand them—someone like Max?

Round and round she went, seeking a sensible way out of all this as the sun finally infused her body with a languorous warmth. Eventually she began to doze when suddenly the raft tilted crazily.

She sat up quickly—and saw Max clinging to its side as he pulled himself out of the water. She failed completely to consider her own attire—or lack thereof—as she stared at his long, lean, muscular body. Thoughts of Otto's papers evaporated quickly in a flush of feminine warmth.

"You made it without a wet suit," she exclaimed as he pulled himself up onto the raft.

"Like swimming in a bathtub," he said dryly.

His eyes remained peculiarly locked on hers, and it was for that reason that she remembered she wasn't wearing a top. In the same instant, a not completely unpleasant sense of vulnerability was added to the rush of warmth produced by his presence.

"Would you be more comfortable if I put on my top?"

He chuckled easily, but his eyes remained carefully on hers. "It's your raft, lady."

Annelise hesitated, suddenly feeling acutely embarrassed but not wanting to admit it. Max sounded entirely too uncaring about the matter, and despite her feeling of discomfort she wanted to find out just how real his blasé attitude was.

In fact, Max's whole attitude toward her was annoying. He was unfailingly pleasant and friendly but nothing more. She hadn't thought much about it because of her preoccupation with Otto's papers—but now that she *did* think about it, she began to wonder.

"How's your work going?" she inquired politely, at the same time unconsciously drawing her knees up to her chest in a self-protective gesture.

Max groaned as he stretched out on the raft beside her and thanked God she had at least done that much to cover herself. It was going to be damn hard to carry on anything like a normal conversation with her today. "Slowly. That man must have saved every scrap of paper he ever put a pencil to. I haven't yet come across the work I've been hoping to find."

Annelise said nothing for a moment. Was it possible that Max could be seeking the papers hidden in the painting? How could she find out? The question made her almost forget her seminudity.

"Have you gotten through it all yet?" she asked finally.

"Yes—in a cursory fashion. I've found some indication that he actually had been working at one time in that area, but nothing of value."

"Otto probably jumped around a lot," she said.

"Oh, he did—but even in the disarray of those papers, I can see some direction to his work."

"Exactly what is this work you're seeking?" she asked.

Max laughed. "I don't think you want to hear it 'exactly,' but its practical application could one day be of enormous benefit to the space program. If we're ever going to be able to travel beyond the confines of our own solar system, we need a different means of propulsion from those now available."

Annelise tilted her head back to stare up at the blue heavens. "Otto was fascinated with the idea of space travel."

Perhaps, she thought, the papers from the painting aren't the ones he's seeking, after all. Otto would never have hidden anything that could benefit space exploration.

Then, abruptly, she remembered the dilemma: great good *and* great evil.

Still staring at the heavens, she asked: "Could it be used for anything else?"

Max was silent for so long that she finally lowered her gaze, then turned to him questioningly. He looked very serious—and also very uncomfortable.

"That's hard to say. I'm not the one who would make that decision. Like I told you, I'm just one of the idea guys."

"Wouldn't you care what your discoveries were used for, Max?" she asked as casually as she could.

"Of course, I'd care," he said rather defensively. "But I'd never withhold a discovery just because I thought it might be put to uses I didn't agree with."

"That's a cop-out, Max," she stated firmly. "If they're *your* discoveries, then they're *your* responsibility."

Max looked at her, wondering uneasily if she *did* know, after all, what those papers contained. But how could she?

"I don't see it that way," he replied. "It's my responsibility to pursue knowledge—wherever it leads me."

Annelise was clearly disappointed; he could see that. And in truth, Max wasn't quite so certain about his own feelings on the subject as he sounded.

She had turned away from him and was staring off toward the house. Max in turn stared at her naked back, letting his gaze linger on the gentle curves until he could stand it no longer. She was tormenting the hell out of him. At the moment, in her almost naked state, she had a poignant vulnerability that he'd glimpsed only fleetingly before.

Vulnerability had never been a quality he'd found particularly interesting in a woman—but in this way as in every other, Annelise was different. It was, he thought, those contrasts again: an undeniably strong woman who could also exude a touching vulnerability.

He wanted her. In fact, at the moment, there was nothing else he wanted more in this world than to wrap his arms around her naked, sun-warmed skin. And he was uneasily aware of the possibility that having her might not stop that wanting—or might even increase it.

She had shifted her gaze to the far end of the lake, and now turned abruptly to him, pointing off in the direction in which she had been staring.

"Look, Max! You haven't seen them yet, have you?"

Max sat up and followed her pointing finger. "What?" he asked, still amazed by her ability to act nonchalant while sitting next to him wearing almost no clothes.

"Loons." She said, then began to laugh as another bird came in for a landing. It hit the water with what seemed to be great force, bounced a few times, then finally settled down.

"I've seen films of them, but this is the first time I've seen the real thing," he said, still grinning.

"Wait until you *hear* them." She smiled. "Early morning and dusk are the two times they generally call."

"Do they always land like that?"

"Oh, sometimes it's even worse. It's not unusual for them to misjudge the amount of space they need for landings and end up plowing into the grass at the edge of the lake."

Then she gave him one of her gamin grins. "One summer when I was little, I became so worried about them hurting themselves when they crashed onto the bank that I carried just about every pillow in the house out here to provide them with soft cushions."

She shook her head with a laugh. "Can you imagine twenty or thirty pillows all lined up along the bank down there? I had just about cleaned out the house when my mother finally caught me."

Max threw back his head and laughed. "I think I *can* imagine it. What a little brat you must have been."

She gave him a mock contemptuous look. "I prefer to think of it as being resourceful."

They sat there side by side watching as the loons upended themselves in their search for fish. But the birds were nothing more than a distraction. Annelise was by now very uncomfortable

67

with her near nakedness, and Max was thinking that the icy swim back to shore was rapidly becoming an absolute necessity.

Annelise was feeling far too exposed—too vulnerable. Max was making her nervous—intruding into her space. But at the same time, she certainly didn't wish him gone.

She turned her back on him and reached for her bra top, then fumbled nervously with the clasp. Warm fingers touched her bare skin and she let out an involuntary gasp.

"Let me do that for you," he said, his voice rather husky and very close to her ear.

She swept her long hair out of the way, and after he had fastened the clasp, he smoothed it back into place.

"Thank you," she replied, and found her own voice embarrassingly husky, too.

He removed his fingers, but didn't back away. She didn't turn, but could still sense his closeness. For a moment, she was sure that he would touch her again; she could almost feel his strong arms close around her. But the moment hung suspended in the charged atmosphere—and then she shattered it by getting to her feet.

"We can race for shore as soon as you've had enough time to warm up," she suggested with false brightness. She was eager to get back to the house and into more clothes—and to resume that "lady of the manor" role she had temporarily let slip away.

"I'm ready," he replied. "If I could manage a swim in the Antarctic, I can handle this."

She turned to him in surprise. "The Antarctic? You mean that place at the bottom of the world—penguins and all?"

Max nodded. "I went there a few years ago with an expedition, in what is loosely termed their summer season. Even though we were all rather well insulated with alcohol at the time, it was still a very short swim."

Annelise laughed and shook her head as she turned around to look down at him. "Why do you do such things—caving, climbing and the rest?"

Max shrugged. "From the time I was a kid, two things have fascinated me: science and adventure. For a while, I thought I might combine them in some way, but when my science interest narrowed down to physics, I knew that wouldn't work. So I just divide my life between them."

"Indiana Jones," she pronounced, shaking her head mirthfully.

"That analogy has been made before," he admitted, "Even by my department head, who questions my commitment to my profession."

"But not enough to prevent you from getting tenure, surely?"

"Oh no, they gave me that. But there is still a suspicion that Max Armstrong isn't committed to academia to the extent that he should be, and there are occasional grumbles to the effect that I could prove them wrong by giving up my summer vacations to science."

"Since you're here, does that mean that you've decided to placate them?" she asked.

"No. First of all, I'll be giving up only a small part of my summer, and secondly, this is something I'm really interested in."

Annelise was silent. He had never been specific about the duration of his stay, but now she recalled that Hilde had foisted him upon her by telling her that he wouldn't be here long. She was no longer happy about that.

Then she thought: All the more reason to delay any decision about those papers. If they are what he's looking for, and I give them to him, he might leave.

Annelise discovered, somewhat to her dismay, that Max Armstrong was moving closer to the edge of her space, and that she just might be willing to let that space shrink a bit.

But not too quickly, she counseled herself. Just keep him around and wait to see what develops.

She stepped to the edge of the raft and prepared to dive. "I get a head start to compensate for my size."

"But . . ." was all she heard of Max's protest as she dove into the icy waters, and immediately struck out for shore. A few seconds later, she heard a splash as Max too hit the water.

Unbeknownst to Max, Annelise was a very powerful racing swimmer. She'd been the star member of her school's championship team. She was looking forward to clambering out onto the bank and waving at him as he labored toward shore.

As usual, she managed to reach the halfway point before feeling the full effects of the icy water. In all her years of swimming in the lake, she had never once suffered from the muscle cramps that can affect those swimming under such conditions. But the fates were not so kind this day.

A sudden and painful cramp struck her left calf, and she faltered. As soon as she was, in effect, immobilized, the chill of the water was magnified. She struggled to tread water, while at the same time massaging the cramped muscle. For one brief, horrifying moment, she thought she might actually drown.

Then a powerful arm encircled her and began to draw her along. The irrational fear subsided quickly and she resisted the urge to grab on to him, instead letting him hold her as he pulled them both along.

Just before they reached shallow water, the cramp eased up a bit, and by the time she could set her feet onto the sandy bottom, the pain had settled down into a dull throb. Max's arm still encircled her as they both hurried out of the water.

She was shivering violently from the shock of the prolonged exposure to the water, and she could actually hear her teeth chattering, something she'd never quite believed really happened.

Max left her standing there, too miserable to move, and grabbed the long terry robe she had left by the shore. He helped her into it, and disregarding his own discomfort, began to massage her through it.

"Th-that n-never h-happened before," she said disbelievingly.

Max continued to rub her gently, his face full of concern. "Well, it did this time, and it's a damned good thing I was there." His voice was almost rough, and caused her to draw back a bit.

"I wouldn't have drowned," she insisted stubbornly, even though a few moments before, she had feared just that.

Then, realizing belatedly how ungrateful she sounded, she softened her tone. "Thank you."

He just nodded and let her go as he pulled on the sweat suit he'd worn over his swim trunks. Annelise stood there and watched him, feeling like a fool.

"I'm sorry, Max. I *did* think for a moment that I was going to drown."

Max pulled the sweatshirt over his head, then stared at her. She stood there in the bright red robe, looking small and miserable. He noticed that her lips were still blue. Without considering the wisdom of his action, he walked back to her and scooped her up into his arms.

"You need something hot to thaw you out inside," he said as he started back to the house with her.

She uttered a small cry of surprise when he picked her up, but didn't struggle. The truth was that it felt very good to be in his arms. It seemed that that all-important space was shrinking even more rapidly than she had thought.

"Chicken soup," she said. "Mrs. M. makes up huge batches and freezes it."

"The all-purpose cure-all," Max agreed with a chuckle. "In no time, you'll be right back to being the lady of the manor again."

She opened her mouth to protest, then closed it again. She was sure he was trying to provoke her into self-righteous indignation and decided not to give him the pleasure. Besides, it was much more fun to enjoy the feel of his strong arms around her as he effortlessly carried her back to Singing Waters.

Max didn't set her onto her feet until they reached the big kitchen, and she felt a pang of regret when their bodies lost contact. Their glances met and she saw that emotion mirrored in his dark eyes, too.

She heated the soup in the microwave, then poured it into two big stoneware mugs. They both settled down at the small table in one corner of the huge kitchen, and Annelise found herself looking everywhere but at Max. She wasn't yet prepared to accept the possibility that things were rapidly moving beyond her control—but neither could she quite push that thought away.

"You're a very good swimmer," Max commented as he sipped his soup.

She nodded. "I swam on a championship team in school. You see, I had planned to dazzle you with my prowess. I imagined myself standing on the shore and waving to you while you were still only halfway."

Max laughed. "Sorry to disappoint you, but I've done some racing, too. In fact, at one point, my coach wanted me to try out for the Olympics."

She frowned. "I was beating you until I got that cramp."

"I was staying behind you to be sure you were okay," he countered.

She glared at him and he returned the look blandly.

"Hilde said you were a gentleman, Max, and gentlemen do not brag."

"Hilde was wrong."

"We'll race another day," she said, getting up from the table after finishing her soup.

"In wet suits," he agreed, watching her with amusement.

She left him in the kitchen and went to change, feeling vaguely annoyed with herself. She hadn't exactly been gracious to a man who might have saved her life, but she was willing to forgive herself for that. What was annoying her was that she had actually enjoyed those moments of helplessness when she'd been in his arms.

Annelise strongly disapproved of helplessness. Through the force of her personality, she'd always managed to control events and the people in her life. Surely she wasn't going to let a mere professor gain the upper hand here.

Later that evening, Max set aside the papers he'd been working on and got up from the desk to walk to the terrace doors. They were open to take advantage of the surprisingly warm evening, and as he stepped through them, he saw that the terrace and the gardens beyond were bathed in the pale silvery sheen of a nearly full moon.

Annelise had vanished after fixing them a remarkably good chicken dish for dinner. That she could cook at all had surprised him, but that she appeared to be a gourmet cook was nothing short of remarkable. It seemed that he was constantly underestimating her and she was therefore continuing to catch him off guard. In fact, he suspected that this demonstration of her culinary skills was somehow related to the incident in the water. Perhaps she felt that he was getting too close to understanding her.

He saw her now at the far end of the terrace, curled up in a big wooden Adirondack chair. If it hadn't been for the moonlight reflecting off the white in her hair, he might have missed her in the darkness.

She was still wearing the outfit she'd worn at dinner: a black skirt that reached nearly to her ankles and an oversized matching shirt, held in at the waist by that gold-scaled snake. Max had read or heard somewhere that artists were very sensitive to colors, and he was inclined to believe it because her mood had nearly matched her outfit. She'd been polite but distant, frequently staring off into space.

Max was disinclined to accept this latest mood change as being normal—even for her. It *could* have been the result of that incident this afternoon; he knew she resented being helpless. But he guessed that what was really troubling her were those papers she'd found.

He'd given some thought to the possibility of confronting her with his own discovery, but had decided against it. Whatever her reason for keeping the papers from him, she was likely to resent any pushing from him.

Annelise heard Max approaching and welcomed the intrusion. She'd been debating the wisdom of telling her Uncle Paul, the head of the family now, about Otto's secret. Paul lacked Otto's gentle humanity, but he also—fortunately—lacked her father's hard-nosed attitudes.

Max came up and stopped before her, smiling. Her bare feet were curled up under her skirt, and she felt her toes curl reflexively. If she didn't watch it, she thought with amusement, she just might start purring. Max certainly brought out some strange feelings in her.

"Would you prefer to be alone?" he asked.

"No, of course not. I just didn't want to disturb you while you were working."

You do that anyway, he thought as he looked down at this woman who seemed so frail and yet so terribly imposing.

She grew nervous under his scrutiny and stood up. "I heard the loons a while ago. Let's go down to the lake," she said, starting across the terrace, and leaving him to follow along in her wake.

He continued to wonder about men in her life and reached the conclusion that there probably hadn't been many. How many men could cope with this fascinating creature for any length of time? And how many would have the patience to wait for her to allow them into her life?

He caught up with her and found himself once again surprised by her small size. Only when he was very close to her did he remember it. The rest of the time, she seemed to fill whatever space she chose to occupy.

Max had known quite a few women over the years who had achieved great success, but he could not recall any who had ever exhibited the presence Annelise had. Neither was he quite certain just how he felt about that.

Annelise was thinking how very calming and reassuring it was to be with Max, and how she'd never considered those qualities to be a plus before, since they seemed only a half-step away from boredom.

They strolled down to the lake's edge and stopped just as the mad cry of a loon shattered the evening's stillness. Both of them immediately began to laugh. But when their laughter had died away, the evening suddenly became oppressively quiet.

It might have been only an accident that his hand brushed against hers as they stood side by side. But it was certainly no accident that he curled his fingers around hers to enfold them in his warmth.

They continued to stand there, staring out at the moon-silvered lake. Max had made the first tentative move and she knew instinctively that he was waiting for some sign of encouragement from her. Such a moment called for some serious thought, but she found that the only thought in her mind at the moment was a memory of how good—and how right—it had felt to be in his arms.

She turned to him, then seized his other hand. He was still looking rather startled when she stretched up on tiptoe and kissed his mouth softly, then quickly backed away.

"I'm glad you're here, Max—even if I was angry when Hilde pushed you at me."

He smiled down at her. "I'm glad I'm here, too—even if I thought I wanted to be in Switzerland instead."

Then he leaned forward, allowing her plenty of time to withdraw or to protest. But she raised her face and parted her soft lips to welcome his. Their mouths clung together with aching tenderness, even as their bodies remained discreetly apart. Max slid his arms about her slowly and carefully, as though he half expected her to protest or perhaps to disappear completely. But the soft, yielding mouth against his and the firm, womanly curves pressed against him were very real.

Annelise stretched up on tiptoe to twine her hands through his thick, wavy hair as his gentle demands met her own growing need. She'd known it would be like this; she'd already sensed that wonderful capacity for tenderness in Max.

Gradually, the careful explorations began to turn into sensual demands, and two bodies strained for a closeness denied to them by layers of clothing. There was a small hesitation on both their parts, and then they slowly withdrew, leaving a silence in which each of them could hear the rapid beating of their pulses.

Max ran a thumb caressingly across her kiss-swollen mouth and gave her a rueful grin. "Moonlit lakes can be very dangerous," he said huskily.

"And the moon isn't even full yet," she replied softly.

At that moment, the loons began their raucous laughter once more, and they both joined in. Each of them swore silently that there was mockery in that wild laughter.

CHAPTER FIVE

It should not have been difficult for them to avoid each other in a house as big as Singing Waters. When he'd first arrived, Max had soothed himself with that very thought. And Annelise had agreed to his visit only because she knew they could stay out of each other's way in the huge house.

Singing Waters remained just as large, but each of them was constantly aware of the other's presence. Distance didn't matter, either. Max began to go for long trips through the woods on his motorcycle when he wasn't working on Otto's papers, and Annelise continued her solitary treks through the forest when she wasn't hard at work in her studio.

And yet . . . Max would park the bike and settle down in the quiet of the forest, several miles from her, and still feel her presence so strongly that he wouldn't have been surprised to see her suddenly appear before him.

And yet . . . Annelise would suddenly discover that the paint on her brush had dried while she stood before her canvas, lost in a memory of that kiss.

Neither of them was an innocent; both had known desire. But far beneath the attempts to dismiss these lapses as nothing more than that lay the rising certainty that this is different.

Max regularly reminded himself of the reasons why this should go no further: her eccentric, strong-willed nature that could wreak havoc upon the stability of a relationship, her wealth that would almost certainly drive a wedge between them at some point.

Annelise deliberately dredged up all her contempt for the stuffiness of the academic world, but each time she did an annoying inner voice suggested that maybe this man was different. In desperation she switched to thoughts of the iron will she thought she detected beneath his easygoing exterior, a will that might very well match her own.

And they both worried about what to do with the secret that lay between them. Max wondered if she might have destroyed those papers; such a move wasn't beyond the realm of possibility, given her unpredictable and impulsive nature. By now, he had gotten through enough of Otto's work to know those missing papers contained evidence of a startling and important breakthrough.

While he fretted about their possible destruction, Annelise worried about what to do with the papers that remained hidden in her drawer. She was virtually certain by now that she had the papers he sought. She feared that her failure to turn them over might drive Max away, but to do so could well mean betraying the trust Otto had placed in her.

By now, after considerable thought, Annelise had decided that she understood what had happened. Otto had probably secreted the papers behind the painting years ago—perhaps shortly after she had given it to him. As she recalled, that discussion they'd had about scientific responsibility had come not long after that. Possibly he had intended to wait it out, to see if some other physicist made the breakthrough and thereby resolved the dilemma for him.

But time had run out for Otto, and had run out so abruptly that he'd never had the chance to explain it to her. He might even have attempted to do so during his final, agonizing days in the hospital. His speech had been severely affected by the stroke, and she might have been so lost in her own misery over his illness that she hadn't even heard his attempt to explain. Or perhaps by that time he himself had forgotten all about it.

On a miserable, rainy day that had kept them both indoors and therefore too close to each other for comfort, Annelise interrupted Max's work to inform him that she intended to prepare boeuf bourguignon for dinner. Max reminded her that they had finished off the last of the burgundy several evenings before.

"Oh, there's bound to be plenty in the wine cellar."

"I didn't even know there was a wine cellar," Max commented.

"Well then, come along and see. Otto was the family wine expert, and he maintained quite a collection."

He followed her to the kitchen, where she paused to take a key from a cabinet.

"You keep it locked?" he asked in surprise.

She laughed. "Family tradition—a fairly recent one, though. One summer, Otto announced that he was locking it because he'd caught several of my older cousins messing around down there and he suspected they were sneaking drinks.

"Since the wines were his no one objected—except for my cousins, of course—and they were in no position to protest.

"There's no reason to keep it locked now, of course, but we've just continued to do so."

She paused to unlock the door, then pushed it open, to be immediately assaulted by the aromas that somehow managed to escape from the corked bottles.

The wine cellar had been a favorite hideout of hers as a young child. She loved the fruity smells and the racks of bottles gleaming in the light of two overhead bulbs. But for many years, she'd come down to the wine cellar only rarely. Somehow, it had seemed wrong to be drinking Otto's wines—as though once they were gone, Otto himself might be gone.

She flipped the light switch and stared at the racks that lined all four walls of the small room. That strange sensation was back again, and she supposed that she'd never get over it. Sometime after Otto's death, when she'd come down here for the first time in her adult life she'd had the weirdest feeling that the room had become smaller by some immeasurable amount. It was, of course, the difference between seeing the room through an adult's eyes as opposed to those of a child, but that eerie feeling persisted to this day.

Max roamed around the room, pulling out bottles at random to examine them. "You know, you could have one of the world's greatest collections of expensive vinegar down here by now."

"Yes, I know. But the few we've had have been fine."

She located several bottles of burgundy. Max frowned at them. "Burgundys are supposed to be drunk young."

"We aren't *drinking* them," she reminded him. "If they've gone bad, I'll change the menu."

They left the wine cellar and Max walked down the dimly lit hallway. "What else is down here?"

"Just the boiler room, some storage rooms, and the billiards room."

"Billiards?" he echoed, then stopped as he came to the room in question.

She followed him, wrinkling her nose in disdain. "Not one of my favorite games."

Max picked up the cover to peer at the table. "I'll teach you."

"I'm afraid that's been tried several times. Otto and Paul used to play, and this was the one room where they were permitted to smoke cigars."

They started back toward the stairs again, with Max remarking that he was glad to have learned about the table, since it would provide a pleasant diversion from his work.

"By now, I'd have thought you would know the whole house," she commented, having assumed that he'd explored it all.

"No, it never occurred to me to come down here. I haven't seen the upstairs family wing, either."

There was a momentary pause in the conversation as she glanced at him questioningly.

"I didn't want to intrude," he hastened to add.

She said nothing as he followed her up the stairs. Max began to feel slightly hurt. He'd thought—or hoped—that his status had advanced somewhat beyond that of houseguest, but her silence seemed to indicate otherwise. They walked into the kitchen, where she set the bottles on a counter, then turned to him with that smile that transformed her into a pixie.

"It's my fault. I should have offered to show you the rest of the house—especially the master suite. That was Otto's, and I think you might find it interesting. Come along."

She left the kitchen and Max followed her, then frowned as she failed to start up the staircase. Without a word, she led him back to the library.

As he stood there in the doorway, looking perplexed, Annelise walked purposefully over to one of the bookcase-lined walls and reached out to remove a large volume. Then she reached into the empty space where the book had been.

Suddenly, a large section of the bookcase began to move forward with a screeching, rasping sound. Max reacted with lightning speed, grabbing her roughly and hauling her away from the falling bookcase. Annelise made a startled sound that quickly turned to laughter, even as he saw what had happened.

The forward movement of the bookcase had stopped. It shuddered lightly on the concealed hinges which had opened it like a door. He looked from it to her with a bewildered expression, still holding her to him tightly.

"What the hell . . . ?"

She laughed again, but he heard the slight huskiness this time and immediately lost interest in whatever secret the bookcase might be concealing. No secret Singing Waters might contain could possibly fascinate him as much as the woman he held in his arms.

He loosened his grip on her upper arms slightly, then began to caress the delicate skin. "Did I hurt you?"

She shook her head with a smile. "As a matter of fact, I think you might come in handy if I ever *were* in danger."

They smiled at each other in mutual acknowledgment that "danger" could take many forms. Then they moved apart rather self-consciously and very reluctantly.

"Where does this go?" Max asked as he stepped around the edge of the bookcase to peer into the dimly lit staircase beyond.

"To the master suite, of course," she said as she followed him. "The light at the top must be burned out. They're both supposed to come on when the bookcase is opened. Those hinges must need oiling, too. I doubt if anyone's been in here since Otto died."

She stared into the darkness doubtfully. "How long do you suppose spiders could live in here?"

Max turned to her with a grin. "Spiders?"

"Yes. If no one's been in here for five years, they've probably taken over. I am not fond of spiders."

Max started up the narrow stairs. "In that case, I'll risk death to shoo them away."

She followed him. "Big hairy spiders, Max—with teeth like piranhas."

"I've had some experience with piranhas, so I think I can handle it," he said, and shrugged.

He reached the top and stopped on the narrow ledge before a door. The burned-out bulb left the area in almost total darkness.

"How do you open this door? I can't find the knob."

She stepped up beside him, once again very much aware of his closeness. "It's not a knob; it's a sliding panel."

She began to feel around for the latch that would release the door, and Max circled her waist as she tottered on the narrow top step. Annelise began to think that this might not have been such a great idea, after all. What would he think when she showed him Otto's favorite addition to the suite? She knew what *she* was thinking.

"Ahh, there it is." With considerable relief, she located the latch and slid the door open.

They stepped out into what Max saw was a dressing room—

82

oak-paneled with closets lining two walls. Annelise opened the door in the opposite wall and went through.

"Paul uses the suite now, since he's the senior member of the family. Hilde is actually two years older than Paul, but she's a mere woman. The family hasn't quite advanced into the twentieth century. I'm trying to organize a rebellion for my generation, since the two oldest are both females."

Max was paying her scant attention as he gaped at the room. He'd thought his own room must be about as luxurious as any, but now he could see he was wrong. If she had told him that the Queen of England stopped here regularly, Max wouldn't have questioned it.

The room was enormous and even contained a small alcove that was apparently a sitting room. Like the main rooms downstairs, it had a marble fireplace, although this one was a dusty pinkish coral. Max guessed that the furnishings in this one room were probably worth more than everything he owned, and the thought was something less than comfortable.

Annelise saw his expression and grinned. "It *is* a bit much, isn't it? You can imagine how that painting of mine fit in."

Max shot her a quick look as the painting reminded him of those papers. "Speaking of that painting, I see that you brought it down from the attic," he said casually. "And broke the frame."

"Oh, no damage was done. I never liked that frame anyway." She hoped she sounded as casual as he did, then moved quickly across the room looking for a way to change the subject.

"Come here, Max. This is what I should have shown you before."

Max came up behind her as she gestured to the room beyond. It was obvious that he'd gotten nowhere with that ploy. But once again, he forgot all about the papers as he followed her sweeping gesture.

"This was Otto's addition to the suite. One is tempted to use the word 'decadent.' "

Max chuckled. The main focus of the large bathroom was a huge marble tub, which he saw had been fitted with a Jacuzzi.

"He claimed that it was very beneficial for his arthritis, but I prefer to think he was having orgies up here when the rest of us weren't around."

Max found himself thinking along the same lines—but without including her late uncle in the scene. He noted too that after her teasing words, she had begun to exhibit those signs of nervousness he'd noted before on occasion.

"You might find this a pleasant way to relax after your motorcycle rides," she went on with false brightness.

Max said nothing, thinking that it might be equally nice to spend some time up here after a candlelit dinner and before . . .

"I imagine you must suffer some bumps and bruises riding that thing through the woods."

"Uh, yes, sometimes. I'll keep it in mind."

She left the bathroom, saying that she had to start dinner, and Max trailed along behind, after casting one last longing glance at the big tub. She walked into the dressing room, then paused at the top of the stairs. Max came to a halt behind her.

"Do you want me to go first?" He asked, thinking that the dark stairs bothered her.

But Annelise didn't hear him. An old, almost buried memory had surfaced—one that had come back briefly right after Max's arrival, when they'd been talking about Otto. She stared down the dark steps. The bottom light bulb had been burned out that night—and then the top one had gone out, too, when the power went off. She shivered involuntarily, and then felt Max's arms circle her waist as he bent close to her.

"Nellie, what is it?" Her nickname just slipped out without conscious intention, since he'd been calling her that to himself ever since the first day. It was so outrageously unsuitable that he found it charming.

"Nothing," she said after a moment, moving quickly down the stairs. "Just a childhood memory."

Curious, Max asked if these stairs had been a hideout for her, too, like the wine cellar.

"No, not really," she said in a distracted tone. "This was Otto's private staircase." But something had happened there, something that even now troubled her. Perhaps that was why she'd tried to bury it so deeply.

Max wanted to pursue the matter because he could tell that something was obviously troubling her, but she gave him no opportunity. As soon as they had reached the bottom, she said she had to see to dinner, and left him in the library. Max looked from her disappearing form to the staircase and frowned thoughtfully. Then he closed the bookcase and went back to work.

As she set about preparing dinner, Annelise continued to think about that memory. How old had she been then? About nine she thought, maybe even younger. It was strange how it continued to trouble her, even though it had all been explained at the time.

It was late that summer, she recalled. Most of the others had already departed, leaving only Annelise and her brother and parents. Her parents had gone out to dinner or to a party somewhere, leaving Annelise and her brother in Otto's care.

She had just fallen asleep when she'd been awakened by one of the violent storms that plagued the region at certain times of the year. The lightning didn't frighten her, but the horrendous booms of thunder that seemed to shake the house did. She'd gotten out of bed, then remembered that her parents wouldn't be there. She'd gone off to the master suite to seek comfort from Otto.

None of the other children would ever have gone to Otto in such a situation, but Annelise knew her high place in her uncle's affection, and after knocking loudly on his door, she'd gone in. The suite was empty, but the door leading into the secret stairwell was open. Knowing he must still be down in the library, she'd hurried down the steps, only realizing when she was partway down that the door at the bottom was closed.

Still, she'd gone down, thinking that she could shout to gain

Otto's attention. But as soon as she'd reached the bottom, she'd heard sounds in the library.

Annelise paused now in her dinner preparations and frowned, trying to recapture the memory completely. But it was so long ago, and there'd been the thunder, loud and terrifying even in the stairwell, and the heavy bookcase had muffled the sounds from the library.

What she'd thought she'd heard that night were angry voices, but later, when she'd asked Otto about it, he'd told her that she must have heard the Wagnerian opera he was playing at the time. Otto had loved opera, and Wagner had been his favorite. Since no one else had been in the house, she'd accepted his explanation. And yet . . .

She shrugged away the memory. Like the diminished size of the wine cellar, it was one of those vestiges of childhood that persisted way past their time.

Max came into the kitchen then, and after sniffing appreciatively, said that he'd oil the bookcase hinges and replace the burned-out light bulb if she'd show him where the supplies were kept. She gestured to the utility room, then turned back to her work.

What was she going to do about Max? They couldn't go on sharing the house without *something* happening between them, she thought. He hadn't yet said anything about when he'd leave, but she suspected it might be soon. He must have examined most of Otto's papers by now.

The thought filled her with something uncomfortably close to panic. She didn't want Max to leave. On the other hand, if he stayed, sooner or later—and probably sooner—something was going to happen.

A pleasant feeling of warmth began to unfold inside her as she thought about that possibility. She knew instinctively that Max would be a wonderful lover. He was warm and gentle and already seemed so well tuned to her moods and needs. He felt right; it was as simple—and as complex—as that. And she also knew that only the subtlest of signals from her would turn them into lovers.

If she were able to think of him only as a summer fling, a pleasant diversion with no strings attached, she might well have sent that signal already. Not that she sent such signals often; in fact, Max and everyone else who knew her would probably be very surprised at just how inexperienced she was. Her free-spirited nature and her forceful personality could easily mislead those who didn't know her well.

To Annelise, lovemaking was the ultimate invasion of privacy, and she guarded that privacy very closely. And if lovemaking was the ultimate invasion of privacy, then marriage was the seal that made that invasion permanent. Marriage meant sharing herself.

There had been one time, a few years ago, when she had considered sharing herself. She'd known the man in question for quite a while and after much indecision had believed that the two of them could build a happy relationship.

He'd moved in with her, and within a month, she'd known it just wasn't going to work. She liked him, respected him, and enjoyed his company, but living together had somehow pulled them apart, instead of drawing them together. They'd parted soon after that, and Annelise had become more certain than ever that she was destined to remain alone.

Now that certainty was wavering very slightly. Her attraction to Max was growing every day. She couldn't bear to think that he might leave, and yet she feared for what might happen if he remained. For all his casual, laid-back manner, Max Armstrong was no pushover. If she let him into her life, she would be dealing with a personality that might very well match her own in forcefulness.

Max was delighted with the dinner she had prepared. After they finished eating and he was taking care of the cleanup, Annelise went to the TV room to find a movie for them to watch. A steady rain continued to drench Singing Waters, punctuated by noisy thunderstorms. She had long since outgrown her fear of storms, but tonight they made her edgy.

Part of that nervousness was the result of that revived childhood memory, but a larger part was her heightened awareness of their isolation here. She'd spent many summers alone at Singing Waters and had never felt isolated before. But now Max had come along.

During dinner, this strange awareness had crept over her stealthily, causing every word and gesture to assume an importance out of all proportion to reality. She had measured her every word with great care—something she'd certainly never done in the past—and had analyzed every utterance from Max with the same attention. There was electricity in the air, and it had nothing to do with the weather outside.

And yet nothing had really changed. Max was the same relaxed, funny, and warm companion he had been from the first. Nothing he said or did could have been construed as indicating a heightened awareness of her—or a growing desire for her.

Still, she knew without a doubt that he was waiting for some sign from her. To his very great credit, he appeared to be waiting with more patience than most men might have had, but that only increased her discomfort still more. An overt pass could have been slapped down in a hurry; Annelise was very good at that. But this quiet waiting was another matter altogether.

She scanned the library of video cassettes and finally pulled out an old favorite: *The Sting*. Perhaps the antics of Newman and Redford could take her mind off that evergrowing tension. Certainly she didn't dare risk one of the romantic films that she might otherwise have chosen for a rainy summer's evening. With a last, regretful look at two of her particular favorites, *Somewhere in Time* and *The Way We Were*, she went to ask Max's opinion on her selection.

She met him halfway between the kitchen and the TV room and thrust the cassette at him almost in desperation. "This is one of my favorites. Do you like it?"

He glanced at the film and nodded. "It's fine with me, but I'd expected you to choose something romantic."

"Why?" she asked almost belligerently.

The smile remained on his mouth and touched his eyes with gentle humor. "Well, there was that excellent candlelit dinner, and it's a dark, stormy night."

"The dinner was candlelit because the power went off," she pointed out. "And that was only for five minutes. If it had stayed out any longer, I would have called George and asked him to start up the generator."

"You *do* have a way of bringing me back to reality," Max said, sighing.

She almost asked him where he'd been before that, but for once managed to curb her tongue. If his patience was beginning to wear thin, she'd best not try it further.

So they went back into the TV room, where Annelise immediately became uncomfortably aware of the big leather lounger that had been Otto's favorite spot for TV-watching. It had never occurred to her that it was easily big enough for two—but she certainly thought about it now.

Studiously ignoring it, she went to the TV set and inserted the cassette into the VCR. When she turned around, she found Max seated in the lounger, watching her with the smallest trace of a smile on his rugged features.

If he'd made one remark or gesture to suggest that she join him there, Annelise was sure that she would have exploded. Just what that explosion might have consisted of, she didn't know—and furthermore, didn't want to guess, either. But in any event, it didn't happen. She seated herself on the sofa rather stiffly, then finally curled herself into a corner as the film came on.

Laughter began to dissolve the tension in the room, and the process was completed by the wonderfully happy ragtime music of Scott Joplin that accompanied the film. Nevertheless, by the time the final credits began to roll across the screen, the atmosphere was changing again.

For a short while, they could ignore that change by discussing the film. But the conversation began to flounder quickly—the first time this had happened between them.

Annelise jumped up and announced that she was going to make herself a cup of tea. Max said he'd have one, too, even though he knew it would be that perfumed herbal stuff she usually drank. He watched her hurry from the room, then smiled.

She was nervous; there was no doubt about it. He would have been less than honest if he hadn't admitted to himself that that knowledge gave him a feeling of pleasure. It couldn't be easy to make this strong-willed, self-possessed woman nervous.

But he was also honest enough to admit that he too was slightly uneasy. There were too many issues still unresolved where Annelise Vandeveldt was concerned. Would he be leaving himself open to future charges of having used her? How did he really feel about becoming involved with a woman like her—so different from others he'd known? And so rich. There was an issue he still couldn't bring himself to confront head on.

But his soul-searching ended the moment she stepped through the doorway, bearing an antique silver tea service. In fact, all thought ended. Max noted wryly that he always had trouble thinking the moment she appeared.

He said nothing as she seated herself on the sofa again and began to pour tea from the gleaming silver pot. He sniffed appreciatively.

"That isn't herbal tea."

"No, it's a very nice Indian tea," she said rather primly, then spooned in the sugar he requested.

When she had finished, she got up and came over to the lounger to hand him the delicate china cup. He reached for it, his eyes locking with hers for a moment in silent invitation. She hesitated, then retreated to the sofa again, but Max had seen that slight hesitation.

Teacup in hand, she cocked her head to listen to the rain. "I hope the weather will improve by morning."

Max allowed his smile to grow slowly. "So do I—including the weather in here."

He thought he saw her color slightly, but he couldn't be sure.

"What do you mean?" she inquired, permitting her gaze to rest on him for only the briefest of moments.

"It seems to me that the atmosphere in here is a bit thick."

Once again, he received nothing more than a quick glance as she continued to focus her attention on the window. But he saw that her posture had become rigid.

"My work isn't going well at the moment. Surely you must have known that artists are moody people."

"They're also poor liars," he stated calmly.

That brought her gaze to him quickly and her chin up defiantly. She fixed him with her deep blue eyes and smiled. "You're wrong, Max. When I lie, I do it with great flair."

"Just as you do everything else." He smiled.

"Indeed. One can't truly be an artist without being eccentric. It's expected, you see—and in my case, it's also natural."

"How very fortunate for you," he replied in an imitation of her dry tone. "Not so fortunate for me, though."

"What do you mean?" she asked uncertainly.

"Well, I've had very little experience with eccentrics. I don't know the ground rules."

Their eyes locked and neither one wavered. Seconds ticked away, measured by two pounding pulses.

"We'd be very wrong for each other, Max," she said, still fixing him with an unblinking gaze.

He nodded, but his gaze didn't waver either. "You're absolutely right."

"And just because we're alone together in an isolated place, it doesn't automatically follow that we have to become involved with each other."

"Right again—in theory."

"What's that supposed to mean?"

He shrugged. "Just what I said. In theory, there's no reason why our surroundings should influence our behavior."

She refused to ask the obvious question, but did look away.

"In practice, however, things *could* be different," he went on.

"Yes," she admitted. "They *could* be."

"This chair is easily big enough for two," he said in a gentle tone.

"I noticed that," she replied.

"I thought you had."

Annelise was vaguely annoyed with him. Why was he putting the onus on her? Why didn't he just get up and come over to the sofa? She waited until she was certain that he had no intention of doing that, then got up to find that her legs were surprisingly shaky.

The few steps to the big lounger might as well have been a mile. In those long seconds, she thought about all the reasons she shouldn't be doing this. But her feet never faltered.

When she stopped beside the chair, Max slid over to one side and reached up to her. She hesitated, looking for any signs of the victorious male in those dark eyes, then seeing none, gave him her hand and settled down on the chair beside him.

He shifted onto his side and continued to stare at her as he ran one hand absently through her hair. "I can't stop staring at you," he admitted with an honesty that warmed her. "I'm afraid that if I even blink, you'll disappear."

She smiled and raised a finger to touch his mouth lightly. "That's entirely possible."

But not now, she thought. There was just no other place she could possibly want to be. She traced the outline of his mouth, admiring its classic male lines, then trailed her finger down to rest it in the cleft of his chin. His hand remained entangled in the heavy black and white mass of her hair. A heat just short of the kindling point coursed through them both, suffusing them with its warmth and promise of passion.

"I think I may be in like with you," he said huskily, his breath fanning softly against her ear.

She laughed throatily. "I think the feeling may be mutual."

"What should we do about it?" he asked as his lips and tongue moved with moist warmth against her neck.

She cupped his face and drew him up to face her, then threaded her fingers slowly through his thick brown hair. "I think we should move very slowly."

"All right," he agreed as he moved his mouth toward hers with an exaggerated slowness that ended when she impatiently pulled him to her.

But they did indeed proceed very slowly. Mouths met and clung and tongues began lazy explorations while their hands sought out each other's shapes. Max cupped a full breast, then rubbed his thumb gently over the hardened nipple that strained against its covering.

But desire remained on a leash—a leash played out to its full, taut length, and then held there by their agreement. Somewhere in those moments, they both sensed a force far greater than either of them had known before, and the knowledge gave them both pause. Then they very slowly began to extricate themselves from each other's embrace.

She stared at him, her blue eyes darkened with passion—and fear. Max knew that she wanted him, but also knew that she wasn't yet ready to admit that or to face the consequences of that need. He reached out to smooth away the tangled mass of hair that had fallen across her face, then kissed her softly.

"I won't push you, Nellie. I've been waiting a long time for you —and I don't mind waiting some more."

She searched his face carefully, at first unsure just what he meant. He couldn't be referring just to the time they'd known each other. Finally, she nodded in understanding. Perhaps she too had been waiting.

CHAPTER SIX

When Max had told Annelise that he didn't mind waiting, he hadn't exactly been telling the truth. But apparently she had taken him at his word. Days passed—and long nights, too—during which she granted him no more than a good night kiss. If she no longer hid behind her lady-of-the-manor façade, neither did she show any inclination to repeat that scene in the TV room.

There were times when Max came within one frustrated breath of scooping her up into his arms and carrying her off to bed. Such a thought would never have entered his mind if he weren't absolutely certain that she wanted him, too. But in spite of her attempts to pretend nothing at all had happened, the truth slipped out in many unconscious ways: a gesture, a glance, a sudden huskiness to her voice.

More and more, he was coming to the realization that what was keeping them apart were those secret papers of Otto's. He guessed quite accurately that she could not bring herself to make love with him and still withhold that discovery from him. With Annelise, it was nothing or everything. Furthermore, since he had repeatedly stated his frustrations regarding those missing papers, he was sure she knew she had what he was seeking.

There were times when he wanted to grab her and shake her until the truth fell out, and then there were other times when he wanted to tell her to burn the damned papers and be done with it, so they could both focus their attention where it belonged: on each other. This last thought had shocked him, since it was proof positive of the depth of his feelings for her.

Caught between these conflicting emotions and rubbed raw by frustration, Max did nothing. If he confronted her with his knowledge of the papers, she might tell him to leave—even though he knew that would hurt her as much as it would hurt him. And yet, if he let things go on as they were, she might simply continue to do nothing about the papers and about him.

Finally, he decided to risk delivering an ultimatum. If she didn't accept it as such, he could always swallow his pride and backpedal a bit. He reached this decision one evening when they were out on the lake in the rowboat, with Max rowing and Annelise perched in the stern, her knees drawn up to her chest and her chin resting on them as she watched his exertions.

"I'm not getting anywhere," he said.

"Are you hinting that I should be rowing, too?" she asked.

"No, I'm talking about Otto's papers."

"Oh."

Max thought uneasily that she looked supremely unconcerned. "They're interesting, but I still haven't found what I came here for, and by now I know it's not there. The strange thing is that the papers I *have* studied show that he *was* working in that area."

She shrugged unconcernedly. "Well, as you've said before, Otto lacked discipline. Maybe he just lost interest."

"Perhaps—but something tells me that he *did* pursue this."

"What something?"

"For one thing, the work I've seen. And for another, those papers of Harrington's. There were letters, you see, including some from Otto. He made several references to it over a one-year period. Do you think that he might have put them somewhere else?"

"I doubt it," she said in a neutral tone. "Surely they would have been found by now."

Max knew her well enough by now to see the tiny traces of

nervousness that a casual observer would surely have missed. "It's a big house," he persisted.

"Yes, but Otto died more than five years ago. Someone would have found them by now—Mrs. M. and the girls when they houseclean, for example."

Max tried not to scowl in frustration. "Well, there really isn't much more I can do without them. I've got the rest of the papers pretty well organized. If your family decides that you want to release them, there are some that might be publishable."

She said nothing, studiously avoiding his gaze as she stared off toward the house.

"That call I received yesterday was from the grad student who's using my place for the summer. He told me there was a cable from my climbing buddies. Bad weather has kept them from climbing so far, so I could still join them."

The silence that followed that announcement was broken only by the splash of the oars in the water. He found it very difficult to row and hold his breath at the same time. Finally, she turned to him.

"I wonder if Otto *might* have hidden those papers. Perhaps we should make a thorough search of the house."

Max let out his pent-up breath and forced himself to suppress a groan. He had just been outconnived by an expert—and the thought did not go down well at all.

"It sounds to me as though you don't care one way or the other if I leave," he said with something very close to petulance. It was close enough, in fact, that he felt an uncomfortable flush of embarrassment creeping over him. What the hell was she doing to him?

"Of course I care," she stated calmly. "But I can't hold you here."

Max stared at her and saw that gleam of challenge in her deep blue eyes. He decided that she was damned lucky they were in the middle of the lake in a small boat.

America's most popular, most compelling romance novels...

Here, at last...love stories that really involve you! Fresh, finely crafted novels with story lines so believable you'll feel you're actually living them! Characters you can relate to...exciting places to visit...unexpected plot twists...all in all, exciting romances that satisfy your mind and delight your heart.

Get one full-length Loveswept FREE every month!
Now you can be sure you'll never, ever miss a single
Loveswept title by enrolling in our special reader's home
delivery service. A service that will bring you all six new
Loveswept romances each month for the price of five—and
deliver them to you before they appear in the bookstores!

Examine 6 Loveswept Novels for

15 days FREE!

(SEE OTHER SIDE FOR DETAILS)

BUSINESS REPLY MAIL
FIRST-CLASS MAIL PERMIT NO. 2456 HICKSVILLE, NY

Postage will be paid by addressee

Loveswept

Bantam Books
P.O. Box 985
Hicksville, NY 11802

"We can start searching the house day after tomorrow," she went on, as though nothing had passed between them.

"Why not tomorrow?"

"Because tomorrow we're going for a hike. I'm going to take you up to the headwaters of the stream that feeds the lake. It should take us the better part of the day."

Max gave up.

Max examined the supplies spread out on the kitchen counter. "What about wine?"

"Well, we could take some, I suppose—but the water is really good. It even has a slight natural effervescence. In fact, a few years ago, some company asked for permission to bottle and sell it. They actually wanted to build a road all the way up to the spring."

She laughed at the memory. "They even suggested calling it 'Vandeveldt—America's answer to Perrier.'"

Max chuckled. "That must have gone over well with the family."

"Oh, it did indeed. If you think I can be haughty at times, you should see my uncle Paul in action. Paul is very aristocratic to begin with, you see: silvered hair and those light blue eyes that are usually referred to as being steely. They did everything but back out of his presence with a deep bow."

As she spoke, she began to gather together the food, dividing it between their backpacks. "You can carry the cheese and the pâté. I'll carry the bread and crackers."

"That seems to be an unfair division of labor."

"All right, I'll take the first-aid kit."

"I have my compass, and just to be on the safe side I'll bring my gun."

"You won't need either one. I hope you realize that I've already made an exception by permitting you to have that gun here at all."

"You have more faith in the fauna of these woods than I do."

"Yes, I do. I've seen bears and even a wolf once—and none of them bothered me."

"Perhaps they just weren't hungry at the moment," Max suggested. "Or maybe they saw that black and white hair and thought you were a two-legged skunk."

She narrowed her eyes dangerously. "Watch it, Max. You're about half a step away from finding out that I have a pretty decent right hook. I took enough teasing about my hair when I was a kid. In fact, I was suspended from school three times for fighting over it. There are several members of society's best families running around Manhattan to this very day with scars from those fights."

Max grinned. "You're awfully small to be a good fighter."

"I make up for it by fighting dirty," she said, and shrugged.

"I can believe it," he said—and did. "But I'm surprised that you weren't thrown out, since you said that you went to a very exclusive school."

"I wasn't thrown out for two reasons. First of all, schools are only exclusive if they can boast an exclusive student body, and the Vandeveldt name assures that. Secondly, Father bribed them to keep me by providing some new gym equipment, the cost of which he reminded me about on a regular basis."

Max leaned against the counter and smiled at her. "You know, you may think more kindly of your father when you have a child of your own one day—especially if he or she turns out to be like you."

"If I ever do have children, I can guarantee you that they won't have a father like mine," she stated firmly. But she glanced away quickly when he continued to stare at her. Ludicrous as it was, discussing even nonexistent children with him made her uncomfortable.

Max would make a wonderful father, she thought and then immediately pushed the thought away. She hadn't even decided to let him into her life, yet here she was, considering him as a candidate for father to children she wasn't even sure she wanted.

"Let's go," she stated as she picked up her backpack.

Max grabbed his pack from the counter and they left the kitchen to encounter the housekeeper, who was just arriving with one of her daughters.

"We're off to the waterfall, Mrs. M.," Annelise announced.

"Shall I have your uncle's tub filled for you when you get back?" the woman asked, and smiled. "There'll be some aching muscles after that trip."

Annelise just laughed, but Max did not miss the slight flush that colored her pale skin.

"Sounds good to me," he said and grinned.

They said good-bye and started out of the house. As soon as they were out of earshot of the housekeeper and her daughter, Max threw her a challenging look.

"She's right, you know. That *would* be a good way to recuperate."

Annelise said nothing, but started to walk faster. Max very wisely decided not to press the matter, but he certainly thought about it.

In a short time, they were surrounded by the vast forest. Although Max had brought both a compass and a map of the region, he soon saw that they wouldn't be necessary. Annelise obviously knew exactly where she was and where she was going. She pointed out familiar landmarks and talked of her treks through these woods with Otto. Max listened in an uneasy silence.

Over the past few days, Max had forced himself to confront for the first time the possibility that Otto might have had something to do with Harrington's disappearance. Once he had learned of the existence of those papers and the fact that Otto had hidden them Max knew that Otto had lied all those years ago when he'd denied that he and Harrington had made any progress.

But could Otto have been capable of murder? The very question sent a shiver through Max. Annelise had painted a vivid portrait of a gentle, warm man, one clearly incapable of foul deeds. And if he should suggest otherwise . . . ?

He glanced at her as they walked side by side through a fragrant grove of pines. In her camp shirt, hiking shorts, and backpack, she looked almost like a young girl. Except for her very womanly curves, that is. He noted the swell of her breasts beneath the partially unbuttoned camp shirt and let his mind wander back to the house and that big marble tub.

It took them more than two hours of increasingly difficult walking to reach the headwaters of the stream. Most of the trip was accomplished in a companionable silence through which ran gossamer threads of carefully suppressed desire. Each time Max helped her to cross the meandering stream or assisted her in climbing over a rockfall, he found it more difficult to release her. And his attention was being drawn constantly to that lightly throbbing pulse point at the base of her throat.

They could hear the waterfall when they were still almost a quarter-mile away, and Annelise quickened her pace, with Max following closely behind.

And then they were there and Max immediately understood why she had wanted to show him this place. He decided that the Garden of Eden might well have looked just like this. The waterfall was about thirty feet high, emerging from a rocky outcropping in the steep side of a hill. It was a gentle, tinkling, gurgling dapple of water that rushed over rocks green with moss. Close to both sides grew enormous ferns and dark, shiny rhododendron bushes. At the base was a small natural pool.

Among the rocks surrounding the pool was a very large flat boulder that provided the perfect vantage point from which to enjoy all this pristine splendor. They unfastened their backpacks and sat down on the rock. The air was fragrant and blessedly cool after their strenuous climb.

"This is wonderful," Max said simply.

"Isn't it?" She smiled. "I've been coming here since I was seven years old. Poor Otto had to carry me part of the way back that first time."

"I trust that your stamina has improved," Max said dryly.

100

She laughed and leaned back on her elbows as she stared up at the waterfall. "I've often thought of painting this place, but I'm not all that good at landscapes."

Max followed her gaze thoughtfully. "Couldn't you capture the essence of it in an abstract?"

She threw him a surprised look. "Max, you're beginning to sound positively artistic."

"Well, couldn't you do that?" He persisted.

"Umm, yes," she said as she began to rummage around in the backpacks and lay out the food. "Maybe. I've thought about it."

"Maybe I *am* getting artistic," he mused as he reached for the loaf of french bread and tore off a hunk. "Sometimes, I even think I half understand your work."

"Oh?" she said with interest. "And what do you see in the canvas I'm working on now?"

Max appeared to be considering as he chewed the bread. "It seems angry to me. Or maybe that's not quite the right word for it. Perhaps frustrated would be better, and uncertain."

She stared at him for a long moment, then turned away abruptly to spread some pâté on a cracker.

"Am I right?" he inquired innocently.

She got up to fill her cup from the pool. "Maybe."

"You're not doing much to increase my knowledge of art," he observed as she sat down again.

"I'm not sure that we're discussing your knowledge of art."

"Oh?"

"Don't attempt to play the innocent, Max. It doesn't suit you at all."

Faced with her very direct blue-eyed gaze, Max felt chagrined. He nodded slowly, fixing her with a very level look of his own.

"All right, suppose that instead I play a role to which I *am* well-suited: Honest Max, who says just what he thinks."

Privately, he qualified that statement even as he was making it. There was the small matter of those papers. But then she was being dishonest about that, too, so he supposed it evened out.

101

She waited calmly enough for him to go on, but he could see a slight nervousness in her eyes before she lowered them to study the assortment of cheeses spread out between them.

"I think you are beyond question the most fascinating woman I've ever met in my thirty-six years of observing the opposite sex. I find your company exciting, if occasionally frustrating, and I can't think of anything in this world that I'd rather be doing right now than sitting here with you." He paused for effect.

"Except for one thing, that is—and I'm *not* talking about mountain-climbing or caving."

She shot him a quick look, then resumed her contemplation of the cheeses. But he saw her smile faintly and noticed that that faint flush had crept back into her skin. Still, she said nothing, and finally, in frustration, he spoke again. "Isn't there anything you'd care to say?"

She selected some cheese, put it on a cracker, and then finally looked at him. "We haven't known each other for very long, Max."

"So? Is there a timetable somewhere that I don't know about? What is it—handholding for the first two weeks, good night kisses for the next . . . ?"

"No, there's no timetable. But we should feel comfortable with each other."

"Comfortable? What you call comfortable, I call being frustrated. And I'm not alone in that, either. But I can see that this discussion is going nowhere, so I rest my case with the following statement: I want to make love to you—with you. Then I want to fall asleep with you curled up beside me and wake up in the morning and start all over again."

After staring at him for an uncomfortably long time, she simply nodded, then quickly settled down once more to her lunch. Max didn't know what to think and felt more frustrated than ever. That nod could have meant nothing more than that she accepted the truth of his words—or it could mean that she agreed with him. After careful consideration, Max decided not to ask.

Trying to pin her down was like trying to capture a will-o'-the-wisp.

During the rest of their lunch Annelise kept the conversation casual, as if totally denying his words. Then they started the long trek homeward. The closer they got to Singing Waters, the more Max's thoughts turned to that marble tub of Otto's—until he carried before him a vision of the two of them enjoying its pleasures—and each other.

In truth, Max was somewhat befuddled by his overpowering need to possess her. The feeling was uncomfortable, to say the least. That sexual chemistry was there, all right—but he knew it was far more than that. What it came down to, he thought, was that he needed to stake his claim to her. He needed that because he still could not quite rid himself of that feeling that she might vanish in the blink of an eye.

Far from satisfying him, this explanation only made him even more uncomfortable, reminding him of his uncharacteristic irrationality on the subject of Annelise Vandeveldt.

By the time they reached Singing Waters, the housekeeper and her daughter had gone for the day. Even George, the caretaker, and his wife had left to visit relatives for a few days. The silence in the big house was deafening; its emptiness somehow both threatening and tantalizing.

They carried their backpacks into the kitchen and emptied them. Max could actually feel Annelise's efforts to maintain a distinct distance between them, and his fantasy began to fade rapidly, even as he wondered what would happen if he just picked her up and carried her upstairs.

Some men, he thought, might do just that, and the longer he waited the more appealing the idea seemed. Eventually he was forced—reluctantly—to abandon it. Knowing Annelise, it would probably backfire and she'd order him off her property after throwing everything at him that wasn't nailed down.

He watched her puttering about the kitchen unnecessarily as she tried hard to ignore him. Indecision was plain in each and every movement, and indecision did not come naturally to this woman. He tried to think of a way to help, but no answer presented itself.

"If you don't mind, I think I'll go up and take advantage of Otto's Jacuzzi." The words "Why don't you join me?" hovered just behind his lips and he willed her to hear them.

But she just shot him a quick glance as she continued to busy herself doing nothing. "Of course I don't mind."

Max stood there for a moment longer, waiting and hoping, still searching for the magic words that would bring her into his arms. But he sensed that one wrong move on his part now could send her running away from him forever. When his hands began to grow itchy, he turned and left the kitchen.

The big tub looked positively sybaritic, and Max felt rather foolish as he shed his clothes and stepped into the steamy, swirling water. But embarrassment turned into pleasure as he sank into the water. Not until the roiling currents began to soothe him did he realize just how tense he had been. The hike certainly hadn't been strenuous for one who was accustomed to the rigors of climbing and caving, but his muscles ached just the same. Maintaining one's self-control was very tiring business, he thought, and grinned wryly.

After keeping his eyes locked on the open door for many minutes in a foolish hope that she might appear, Max tipped his head back against a folded towel and closed his eyes.

The sounds of the water jets must have masked her arrival, but the sheer force of her presence reached out to him, and he opened his eyes just as she bent her head to untie the knot of her long pink terry robe.

His first improbable thought was that he liked her in pink and hadn't yet seen her wearing it. Pink was a little-girl color, but despite her diminutive size there was no doubting that this was a woman.

A second later, the robe had drifted down over her nakedness and puddled about her feet. Max sat transfixed, his heart thudding heavily as she bent to retrieve some hairpins from the robe's pocket. Then, still totally ignoring his presence, she turned to the big mirror over the sink and began to pin up her heavy hair.

For one wildly irrational moment, Max thought he might have become invisible. He felt like a voyeur as he stared at her naked back, where ribs and spine were lightly etched beneath creamy white skin. With an absolute concentration Max followed the line of her spine to its base, then let his gaze roam over the gentle flare of her hips and down along her lightly muscled legs.

She turned around just as he was about to reverse his visual path, and his eyes immediately locked with hers, replacing voyeurism with bold confrontation. He saw in her direct gaze a slight trace of vulnerability—but no more than that. She started toward him, smiling in a way that was at once shy and knowing. Not one word had yet been spoken.

Before Max could rouse himself from his stupor to assist her, she had slipped into the tub, disturbing the water briefly as she settled down across from him. His long legs were sprawled nearly the length of the oval tub, and he felt her softness come to rest against his ankles and feet. He tried to ignore the sensation for a moment as he cast about for something appropriate to say. How did one go about addressing a fantasy come true?

Nothing in Max's life had ever come close to the eroticism of this moment, and the continued silence between them only heightened that effect. The very force of that sensuality held him in thrall. She was actually here—her soft, naked flesh resting lightly against his hair-roughened legs and big, bony feet. Max began to feel too big and too awkward—more wholly new sensations for him.

He wondered what he was supposed to do. For an instant he thought she might want him to treat her naked presence casually, but quickly dismissed the idea as absurd. There was nothing at all casual about that heavy, throbbing part of him that was growing steadily beneath the swirling waters.

"This is really more of a hot tub, you know," she said suddenly in a calm, almost conversational tone. "There are heating coils hidden somewhere. Apparently, Otto liked to stay in here for quite a while."

"Oh," Max said, knowing that at this moment he was incapable of uttering anything more intelligent than that.

A mischievous glint lit her blue eyes. "If I'm making you uncomfortable, I'll leave, Max."

He quickly shook off his stupor and gave her a challenging look. "If you try it, you'll find out just how fast I can move."

She just smiled at that and said nothing as she sank a little lower in the tub, obscuring the view he'd been enjoying of her rose-tipped breasts.

"Tell me," he said with exaggerated casualness, "am I supposed to act as though there's nothing at all unusual about your presence here?"

She shrugged, briefly lifting her breasts above the water line again. "You did a rather good job of that the day on the raft."

"I had some time to prepare, because I could see that you were topless before I swam out. Besides, that water was cold, and that dampened my, ah, enthusiasm."

"This water isn't cold," she remarked in that same neutral tone.

"I've noticed that, and it seems to be getting warmer, too."

She picked up a sponge and began to apply soap to it, ignoring him once again. Max just sat there watching as she lifted herself up again, then began to scrub her neck and shoulders. When she reached her breasts, Max cleared his throat noisily.

"Would you like some help?"

She smiled and turned herself around in the tub until her back was to him. Then she handed him the sponge over her shoulder. His uncoordinated fingers nearly refused to grasp it.

Several strands of her heavy hair had slipped free from the pins and Max tucked them in again before applying the sponge to the back of her neck and then slowly moving it downward. Her hips

106

now rested against his, and her hand had dropped to rest lightly on his knee.

He reached the base of her spine and began to reverse his path, moving more quickly now until he reached her shoulders. She had remained motionless, but he could sense an inner tension that matched his own.

Then he tossed the sponge aside and began to massage her with soap-slicked hands, gliding over her shoulders and down along her arms. With a barely audible sigh, she relaxed against him and he curved himself around her, sliding his hands down until his fingertips rested against the curving swell of her breasts. He felt her raising herself up, inviting further exploration, and he cupped her breasts. He paused there, savoring a moment unlike any other he had ever known.

From the moment Max had first touched her, Annelise had felt bombarded by sensations she had never known and had never even believed possible. His touch was both gentle and hesitant, but she knew instinctively that his hesitation wasn't born of uncertainty. He too was feeling this moment keenly, drawing from it every nuance of feeling.

When he'd left the kitchen, his unspoken invitation hovered in the air. She'd tried very hard to ignore it, but it refused to go away, and she finally asked herself why she was trying so hard *not* to want Max. Whatever she decided to do about Otto's papers, there was no doubt at all in her mind about what she wanted to do with Max. The future could take care of itself, one way or the other. This was here and now, and it felt right.

Still, by the time she had entered the bathroom, Annelise was already having second thoughts. But his stunned silence had spoken to her far more eloquently than any words might have done. Max was real, as real and honest as any man she had ever known. He was totally devoid of the usual male bravado that made vulnerability totally unacceptable. For all her adult life, she had sought just such a man.

107

So, although Max would never know that, the glibness he had sought would have been his undoing.

A tiny, half-strangled sound poured forth from her involuntarily as his fingertips glided down over her breasts, kneading, shaping, teasing her nipples into achingly sensitive pebbles. He was on his knees behind her now, cupping her breasts as he lowered his head to brush his mouth against her neck and shoulders.

Arching back against him, Annelise reached up to tangle her fingers in his hair. At the same time, her other hand slid over his leg until it encountered the unmistakable evidence of his desire. Her breath caught in her throat and she hesitated.

"Yes," he breathed against the curve of her neck. The one word was drawn out almost as a groan—or a plea.

Her movements were awkward because of their positions as she caressed him. He moved, leaning against her still more, and his hands slid down over her until he found the center of her desire and began to probe her melting, womanly softness.

Passion flared abruptly to an all-consuming fire. They urged each other on with sounds and words until the fire's heat became intolerable and an explosion threatened. Then they climbed out of the tub, shivering in the coolness as Max wrapped Annelise in an oversized towel.

Then he swept her up into his arms and strode out of the bathroom, feeling the incomparable exultation of fantasy become reality. He paused briefly as they came into the master bedroom.

"My room," she said huskily. That seemed right, since she'd spent so many nights there dreaming of this moment while trying to deny it.

So he carried her there and deposited her on the deep blue satin bedcover that was a near-perfect match for her eyes. The towel had slipped a bit and she huddled into it, shivering because she was still wet. Ignoring his own uncomfortable dampness, Max began to rub her with the towel, coaxing warmth back into her body and then feeling that warmth become rekindled passion. He let her go then and began to dry himself impatiently, his dark eyes never leaving her. A tiny part of him continued to fear that she might vanish before his eyes.

Annelise dropped the towel that was partially covering her nakedness and got off the bed to pull down the covers. Then she turned to Max.

They faced each other in silence, neither of them moving—both of them aching with need and fired by the knowledge that that need would soon be met.

Finally, when he could bear it no longer, Max groaned deeply and picked her up again to lower her onto the bed. Then he covered her with himself. She shuddered at the sudden contact with his hard, hair-roughened body, then arched herself demandingly against him.

"You're the impatient one now," he whispered, enjoying the thought.

"Yes," she moaned as she slid her hands around him to force him to her.

But he resisted her and held himself tantalizingly above her. "I haven't had the chance to kiss you properly yet."

Before she could reply, he lowered his face to hers and captured her mouth with soft persuasiveness. When he pushed his tongue into her mouth in sensual exploration, she arched against him again. But he grasped her thrusting hips and held her motionless as the kiss went on. She moaned as she felt him hovering there, his male hardness poised at the very threshold of her female softness.

Then, finally, he raised his head and stared into her passion-darkened eyes as he very slowly glided into her. It seemed to take both forever and just an instant until he had filled her completely. The ancient rhythms took over then, possessing them both, driving out all awareness of themselves as separate beings, and finally bringing them together to that quaking, elusive moment when they truly were one.

They both tried desperately to cling to that moment, but it slipped slowly away, leaving in its wake small ripples of receding ecstasy that gradually became a lingering warmth and a need to be held and soothed.

Max resisted the urge to crush her to him in an effort to recapture the perfection of that moment. Only the certainty that it could—and would—happen again kept his caresses soft and gentle.

Annelise clung to him, fighting desperately against the rising panic that was driving out that warmth. Had she made a mistake? Even as she sought the comfort of his arms, she was wondering if she should try to back off and think this over.

CHAPTER SEVEN

Max felt as though he were awakening into a dream. Her hair was spilled across both pillows, and a few strands were tickling his cheek. Her soft curves pressed against him as they lay together in the bed, and when he drew his first waking breath, her scent filled his world.

He wanted to stretch, but he kept himself still, not yet ready to waken her. A replay of their long night of passion ran through his mind.

After their initial lovemaking, they had roused themselves from bed long enough to throw together a light dinner, which they ate before a fire in the library, both of them clad only in bathrobes. The night hadn't really been cool enough to warrant a fire, but she had wanted one, and he had been happy to oblige. In fact, if she had wanted to dine beneath a palm tree, he would have found one somewhere.

Sometime during their leisurely dinner, Max had begun to sense an attempt on Annelise's part to pull back once more behind her formidable defenses. But he had staked his claim in the most primitive sense, and he was fully prepared to defend that claim. So he had simply ignored her attempts to draw that line around herself again.

Then, when she had persisted, he had simply stared at her until her attempts at casual conversation faltered. At that point, he had just reached over and released the prim knot in her bathrobe tie to bare her to his gaze. Then he had told her in considerable

111

detail just how she had pleased him, how he knew he had pleased her, and how that had been just the beginning.

Somewhat to his surprise, it had worked. She had dropped her attempts to reestablish that space between them and had quickly become once again the incredibly passionate woman who had so delighted him.

Sometime during the night, they had both awakened to a brief moment of disorientation and then rediscovered each other. The flames had burned more slowly then, but no less brightly, and sleepiness had loosened any lingering inhibitions.

Max smiled to himself now as he wondered if he had left so much as one square inch of her delightful body unkissed. Never in his life had he known a woman to be so totally, completely responsive.

And true to her nature, she hadn't been content to react. She had learned about him with astonishing speed and unerring accuracy, seeking out with sure caresses all the sensitive places and sending ripples of pleasure through him that had fanned those flames still higher. Even now, his body retained a pleasurable memory of the tiny prick of her nails and the feather-light touch of her fingers and mouth.

He sighed happily, stretched his long, lean body, and buried his face in the curve of her neck.

Annelise floated back to consciousness very slowly, vaguely aware of the fact that something was very different this morning, and that it might not be wise to think too much about that difference just now. Besides, it was very easy to concentrate on sensation rather than thought.

She lay on her side, half-curled and almost surrounded by him. She knew he was already awake, but didn't acknowledge that fact. She could feel his muscles flex, then relax, and his breath fanned the sensitive skin of her neck as his mouth brushed against her softly.

You are in very big trouble, Nellie Vandeveldt, she told herself. In a moment of weakness, you let this man into your life, and now you aren't going to be able to get him out again. He's here to stay, whether or not he knows it yet and whether or not you are ready to face the consequences.

For a moment, she wanted to scurry out from beneath the covers and run for her life. Perhaps she even made some sort of movement, because even as she thought it, his arm tightened about her waist, and she was drawn back against him still more tightly. And then the thought of leaving just evaporated in a wave of renewed desire as she felt that telltale hardness pressing against her demandingly.

"Good morning," he murmured huskily against her bare shoulder. "Did you sleep well?"

"Yes," she answered, knowing there was no point lying about it.

He turned her over onto her back and loomed above her as he propped himself up on one elbow. His hair stuck out in spiky disarray; his face was stubbly with whiskers, and she thought that he looked just right.

For Annelise, this was the most frightening thing of all: this sense of utter rightness. The simple fact was that Max felt *right*—that being here with him after the most glorious night of her life seemed absolutely correct.

She reached up and stroked his bristly cheek, and he grinned ruefully. "Maybe I'd better get up and shave."

A surge of something very close to panic flooded through her—even though she had been contemplating running away only a few moments before. "No," she said quickly, and then, embarrassed, amended that. "Not yet."

His gaze became even more intently focused. "If I don't, you could end up with a rash—all over."

Involuntary tremors ran through her, and she tried to cover them by stretching. But he had felt them and chuckled softly.

"It's too late, Nellie. You can't back away now. Last night, all those walls came tumbling down, and they're going to stay down."

Then, to prove his point, he began to stroke her as his mouth closed demandingly over hers. His fingers unerringly found all her most sensitive places, and a bright spark of desire grew from the ashes of the night just past.

She made a small, strangled sound that was half protest and half acknowledgment of rekindled need. Then she gave herself up completely to passion. Her body writhed with need, and she touched him as he touched her, feeling an answering surge of desire course through him.

That first time, she had been the impatient one; later, he had staved off his own need to bring her along with him. But by now, their bodies were in some mysteriously wonderful way becoming attuned to each other. Need flowed smoothly into desire and the molten river of desire flooded into a brilliant, shattering climax that carried them both along on its crest.

"You've got to be kidding!" Max stared at her in utter astonishment.

"But I'm not, Max. If Otto wanted to hide something, what better place than in one of these musty old books that no one ever reads? Even Mrs. M. wouldn't have found them when she dusted." Annelise gestured again to the nearly floor-to-ceiling bookshelves.

He might have hidden them in your painting, Max thought but said nothing. His exclamation had said it all. She had spent the remainder of the morning and the early part of the afternoon in her studio, while he had tried to work in the library as he waited with increasing impatience for her to decide to bring the papers to him. When she had finally appeared, he had foolishly believed she was ready to admit that she had them.

Instead, it was now apparent that she intended to continue this ridiculous charade. Max felt angry and hurt. Apparently, she trusted him enough to let him share her bed but not enough to let him have the papers.

She had her back to him as she walked about the library, peering at the book-lined shelves. No doubt she had already calculated just how long it would take to remove each book and riffle through its pages, seeking something that wasn't there now and never had been there.

He threw her an exasperated look. What did she hope to gain by this—a day or two at the most?

She turned around to face him, and his annoyance just dissolved. Perhaps, after all, she needed that time. He remembered her confused look this morning after they'd made love again.

Since the day he'd met her, Max had been aware of the terms on which Annelise Vandeveldt confronted the world. Her unique beauty and force of personality, plus that very blue blood that flowed through her veins, had permitted her to dictate those terms.

It wasn't really fair or accurate to say that she was spoiled, because he'd already seen much evidence of her essential kindness. But still, she and she alone had obviously dictated the course of her life to date, and that confusion he'd seen signaled an awareness that that state of affairs might not continue. Probably, he should be flattered, rather than annoyed, he told himself.

"Well, do you want to look or not?" she asked.

"In a minute," he replied, pushing back the desk chair and holding out his arms to her. "Come here."

She hesitated, then walked over to him, and he drew her down onto his lap. "How did your painting go today?"

"Not very well," she grumbled. "I'm afraid that you've become a major distraction."

"Do you expect me to say I'm sorry?"

She looked up at him seriously. "Max, that show is very important to me. It could make or break me."

He pressed his lips to her brow. "I'm sorry if the timing isn't right, but I'm not going to disappear."

"Just yesterday, you hinted that you were going to leave if you didn't find those papers," she reminded him.

"Is that why you're so eager to tear the library apart looking for them?"

"No, but if we find them, then you'll have plenty of work to do and maybe I can get some work done, too."

Max thought about that and wondered if she planned to hide them in a book or might already have done so. He'd rather that she'd just be honest with him and hand them over, but if that was what she wanted . . .

"And if we don't find them?" he asked.

She affected a careless shrug. "Then they don't exist."

"And then what?" he persisted.

"That's up to you."

He drew back and gave her an intent look. "Are you trying to say that you don't care if I leave? Because if you are, I don't believe you."

"Has anyone ever told you that you can be very pushy at times, Max?"

"No, because I've never really found it necessary before. You're bringing out all sorts of strange behavior in me."

"Oh?" she inquired, avoiding his gaze by picking at some non-existent lint on her black sweatpants.

"Mm-hmm. I even have this crazy idea that I'd rather spend my summer here with you than go off climbing or caving. That sounds pretty serious, don't you think?"

She looked up at him with a perfectly bland expression and asked, "And then what? Summers end, you know."

Max paused for one heartbeat, then said very firmly. "I think that by the time this one ends, we'll both know the answer to that question."

Then he held his breath, half expecting that she would either protest or run, but she just nodded solemnly. Max wondered what was going on in her head, then decided that he might well be spending the rest of his life asking himself that question.

His thoughts began to turn to the bedroom upstairs, but she

abruptly squelched that idea by jumping up and crossing the room to where a rolling ladder rested in a corner.

"I'll start with the top shelves," she announced. "Just how many pages do you think there might be?"

"I have no idea," Max said, and resisted the temptation to add: but you do.

She set to work and Max got up to do likewise, wondering why he was allowing this charade to go on. As he began to remove books, he mused ruefully that despite their intimacy, she remained in some ways as elusive as ever. Furthermore, all his instincts were telling him that it would always be that way.

"Always" was a word that had crept stealthily into his thoughts. A future that didn't include her seemed unfathomable, but Max also sensed keenly that there were problems to come.

First of all, he was almost certain that there was going to be a battle over the disposition of Otto's papers when she finally did decide to let him have them. And secondly, the thought that Otto might have been involved in Harrington's disappearance just wouldn't go away.

Annelise guiltily watched Max as he patiently sorted through the books. She knew that they couldn't possibly check them all today, so she still had time to hide the papers in one of them this evening.

She knew that she couldn't stall forever, and she also knew that she should be up front about it and just hand them over. But it was so much easier to allow him to find them than to be forced to admit that she just hadn't trusted him enough to bring them to him.

She sighed. Their relationship seemed so fragile, and she didn't want it to be that way. A part of her felt that Max had been in her life forever, but an equally strong part fought that notion. She wished fervently that she had never found those papers or that Otto hadn't left his dilemma to her in the first place. Life was complicated enough at the moment without that additional problem.

By the time they quit for the day, they had checked one entire wall's worth of books and made some progress on the other. Earlier, they had decided to go out to dinner, and the nearest decent restaurant was a long drive from Singing Waters.

So, two hours later, they pulled into the parking lot of a charming old inn that the family frequented during their summers at Singing Waters. They had taken her Porsche, and this time she had suggested that he drive. After they got out of the car, Max looked back at it appreciatively.

"I'm going to talk myself into one of those sooner or later," he said ruefully.

She laughed. "I keep trying to talk myself *out* of it. It seems inhumane to confine a car like that to Manhattan most of the time. It spends most of its life in a garage, except for trips up here and occasional trips up to Westchester to visit relatives."

Max made a sympathetic sound, but he kept thinking about the kind of wealth that permitted one to keep a $60,000 sports car for occasional jaunts to the country.

His uneasiness increased as they entered the inn, and Annelise was immediately greeted with the sort of deference he'd always thought was reserved for royalty. Max felt utterly superfluous as every eye in the place followed her progress to the best table in the place.

Somehow, he'd grown accustomed to the luxury of Singing Waters—or perhaps he'd just managed to disassociate it from her. But the behavior of others toward her and her casual remark about the Porsche brought him very quickly back to reality.

It shouldn't matter, he told himself, but a small, inner voice mocked that thought.

"Max, is something wrong?" she asked as he stared blankly at his menu.

"No, nothing's wrong," he assured her quickly, and wished that it were true.

Annelise had already guessed accurately just what was bothering him, and once again, the delicate balance of their relationship was made evident to her. She supposed that they could have gone to a restaurant where she wasn't known, but it wouldn't have mattered in the long run. Max was going to have to accept her as she was.

She was well aware of all the challenges she presented to a man and had long ago decided that any man who was unable to meet those challenges just wasn't worth her time. As Max had so correctly surmised, Annelise Vandeveldt met the world on her own terms.

Still, for the first time in her life, she actually *wanted* a man to meet those terms.

By the time they had finished their excellent dinner, she noted that Max had apparently recovered quite nicely. She even noted a wry sort of smile on his face when the waiter presented the bill to *him.*

The big dinner and the long drive combined to make them both tired by the time they returned to Singing Waters. The night was pleasantly warm, and the sky was filled with stars. Just as they reached the front door, a loon called into the stillness. Max took her hand and suggested they go down to the lake.

They seated themselves on the grassy bank, with Annelise between Max's knees and her head resting lightly against his chest. For a long time, they were content just to sit there listening to the loons and the gentle lappings of the breeze-ruffled water.

But contentment began to edge slowly into desire and the quiet stillness of the velvety night took on a sensuality that grew with each moment. Neither of them had really intended to make love there on the bank of the lake—but it happened.

A casual touch became a heated caress and sighs of contentment edged into soft cries of awakened need. They shed their clothing slowly, scattering scraps of cloth around themselves until nothing remained except for two wonderfully sensitive bodies that cried out for fulfillment.

"We really should go inside," she said when it was far too late to do so.

"We will—later," he replied, his breath fanning softly against her bare skin as he kissed her slender curves.

The dark night was alight with fireflies, the loons continued their sporadic, wild conversations, and the air was aromatic with the mingled scents of grass and pine. The heavens poured forth a ghostly, silvered light as Annelise and Max sought and found that incomparable oneness that was still so new to them.

Their cries were startlingly loud in the quiet night, an affirmation of surrender to forces far greater than themselves.

When it was over Max propped himself above her, then bent to kiss her tenderly. She put up a hand to trace the outline of his face and paused at the tiny cleft in his chin.

"Max, I . . ." She faltered, having started to speak without thought, in words that seemed to spring from the magic surrounding them.

He kissed her again. "I know," he murmured.

And they both decided to leave it at that.

"Well, that's that," Max stated, a trace of annoyance in his voice as he replaced the final book. He'd fully expected to find that she had hidden the papers there somewhere before they had started this ridiculous search. Now he didn't know what to think.

Reluctantly, Annelise climbed down from the ladder. She'd finished the upper rows a few minutes before, then had sat there wondering what on earth she was going to do now. She'd had no opportunity last night to hide the papers, and by the time she awoke this morning, Max had already been in the library, working his way through the remaining books.

She glanced at him nervously as he got up and stretched his long body. Would he start talking about leaving again? She didn't really think he'd do it, but was half afraid to call his bluff. On the other hand, if she just handed the papers over, she'd have a lot of unpleasant explaining to do. She felt hopelessly trapped in the sticky web of her own deceit.

Worst of all, she was beginning to look at all this from his point of view. What would he think of a woman who had been very willing to give herself to him but unwilling to trust him? How could she explain herself?

Max was deceptive. His easygoing nature masked a will that just might be as strong as her own. That it could be even stronger was a possibility she did not choose to consider.

She looked at him again to find him watching her with a trace of annoyance on his rugged features. For one brief moment, she thought he might know that she had been hiding the papers, but she dismissed the thought quickly. He couldn't possibly know.

"Well?" he said, a question implicit in his tone.

"Well what?" she asked as she wondered if there was some other place she could hide the papers.

"What other games do you have in mind?"

She frowned at him questioningly, a feeling of fear running through her. He *couldn't* know.

She managed a shrug. "Well, I suppose he could have hidden them somewhere else. I'll have to think about it."

Max just stood there, regarding her with unnerving steadiness. "Do you think that 'somewhere else' could possibly have been inside that painting of yours?"

For the very first time in her life, Annelise Vandeveldt lost her composure. Her mouth dropped open, her blue eyes widened until they seemed to fill her delicate face and she just stared at him dumbly. Max's expression didn't change.

"You know, those papers aren't as important as the reason you've refused to trust me with them."

"H-how did you know about them?" she asked, as she fumbled about, both for an answer and for a way out of this mess.

Max pulled from his pocket a piece of yellow paper—the paper Otto had always used in his work. He held it up for her examination.

"This was attached to the broken frame." His tone was neutral.

After a moment, she nodded slowly, recalling how one sheet had torn away when she'd first discovered them.

"But how did you find it?" she demanded, retreating into a tone of defensiveness.

Max ignored her tone. "I found it because I went up to your studio that day you brought the painting down from the attic. You had gone out for a walk. I went there because I was trying to understand your art, because if your art was important to you, then it was important to me, too."

Although his tone wasn't accusatory, Annelise cringed inwardly. He'd known all along, then—even before they'd . . . She began to back away from him, literally as well as figuratively.

Max's expression hardened. "Knock it off, Nellie. You know damned well that what's happened between us had nothing whatsoever to do with my wanting Otto's papers."

But the walls he had so recently breached were going up once more. Max saw it and felt it and tried too late to stop it. He took a step toward her, but she backed away some more, and her expression became wary. He stopped and gave her an exasperated look.

"Dammit, Nellie—burn those papers if that's what you want!"

"I can't," she said in a near-whisper. "If that's what Otto had wanted, he would have done it himself."

"Frankly, I'm surprised that he didn't—especially after the thing with Harrington."

"What do you mean?" she demanded.

Max hesitated, knowing he'd said too much. His annoyance at her suddenly wary behavior had made him forget his own deception. He searched desperately for a way to backtrack.

"What are you talking about, Max?" she persisted, her tone regaining a measure of its old imperiousness.

Max jammed his hands into the pockets of his jeans and heaved a sigh of resignation. "Otto was questioned after Harrington's disappearance, because Harrington had told some other faculty members that he and Otto were working on something important and that Otto was 'giving him some trouble.' As I understand it, those were Harrington's exact words. He didn't elaborate, but naturally, when he disappeared, the police were curious.

"Otto denied that they had had anything more than the most casual of relationships. The police gave up, and the other faculty members just wrote it off to Harrington's well-established reputation for bragging." Max stopped, praying that she wouldn't press him any further.

But it quickly became apparent that his prayers were not to be answered. Before his eyes, she transformed herself once again into the haughty lady of the manor. She squared her shoulders, tilted her chin upward and fixed him with a freezing gaze.

"Are you suggesting that Otto was lying?"

"He *was* lying, Nellie. I told you about those letters of Harrington's that were found recently. Harrington and Otto *had* been working together." With each syllable, Max felt himself sliding down into a dark, inescapable abyss.

She stared at him in silence for a moment, then abruptly turned away, wrapping her arms about herself as she marched to the french doors. Her haughtiness had vanished as quickly as it had come. Max wanted very badly to go to her, take her in his arms and tell her that none of this mattered. But it *did* matter— to her, at least—and he was very much afraid that she would reject him.

"You deceived me from the beginning, Max," she said without turning. "You even deceived Hilde."

Max heard the pain in her voice and started to move toward her again. But once more, he stopped. This scene had to be played out, it seemed, even if they were both left wounded as a result.

"That isn't true," he protested rather lamely. "I told you about the letters that had been found. And my interest in Otto's work is genuine."

She turned toward him very slowly, her expression giving away less than her voice had. "But you knew more than you told."

"You deceived me, too," Max pointed out, feeling hopelessly trapped in some absurdly childish game.

"I wasn't intentionally deceiving you. I wasn't even sure they were the papers you wanted. Otto had obviously intended for me to have them, and probably had intended to tell me about them at some point. But he died and I was left with papers I didn't understand—except to know that they must have been important."

"*You* didn't understand them—but you knew that *I* would have," Max pointed out.

She looked away. "Trust doesn't come to me that easily, Max. I would have—"

"What you're telling me is that you'd make love with a man you didn't trust," Max interrupted angrily.

"That isn't true," she protested.

Max took a step toward her, his expression threatening. "Is it not true that we have made love—*repeatedly?* And is it not also true that you just said you didn't trust me?"

"You lied, too," she said defensively, backing away from him.

The very air in the room seemed weighted down by their accusations. A wide, yawning gulf seemed to open between them. Each of them wanted to back away from it, but neither one knew how. Their eyes met across that chasm, defiant and pained.

And then, without another word, she turned around and left the library.

Max stared after her, caught in a volatile mixture of anger, pain, frustration and, most of all, helplessness.

He sank into the desk chair and tried to think clearly—something he certainly didn't appear to be able to do in her presence.

He knew that she might very well be destroying those papers right now—destroying work that might take him and others years to duplicate. But, although he was vaguely aware of the fact that he *should* be worried about that, it was nothing more than a minor concern relegated to the back of his mind.

He couldn't even say that they were back to square one. In

fact, he would have been content if they could start over again with no lies between them. But it was too late for that.

Max knew that trust was important in any relationship, but with Annelise, it was paramount. He'd realized almost from the beginning that she was very wary of others.

He knew too that he'd succeeded in getting her to lower her barriers for a little while. Now he feared they were back up again, higher and more impenetrable than ever.

He sat there, drumming his fingers restlessly on the desk as he wondered what she was thinking. Was she deciding to thrust him out of her life? And just what was he going to do if she told him to leave?

Upstairs, Annelise had decided she'd made a frightening mistake. Despite what Max believed, she *had* begun to trust him, and that made it even worse.

She was far too self-confident to portray herself as a woman wronged. She knew perfectly well that Max would never have used lovemaking as a way to persuade her to turn over those papers. But that intimacy had made her terribly vulnerable—and that she just couldn't stand. The only solution was to send him away. If she didn't . . .

She forced those thoughts from her mind and switched instead to the matter of Otto's papers. Max's revelations had stunned her, and for just a moment, terrifying dark thoughts had crept into her mind. But now she began to think more clearly. So what if Otto had lied? It seemed apparent to her now that Otto must have had grave misgivings about his discovery, and when Harrington had disappeared, he had simply seized the opportunity to hide their work.

But no sooner had she resolved that issue to her satisfaction than the matter of Max Armstrong filled her mind again. Max, with that lazy smile, wonderful gentleness, and touching vulnerability that seemed to match her own.

A voice in her mind whispered: *If you send him away, you will have lost far more than you will have gained.*

CHAPTER EIGHT

She saw Max the moment she emerged from the woods onto the path on the far side of the lake. He was sitting on the grass in the exact spot where they'd made love the night before. She came to a halt, knowing that he hadn't yet seen her.

Why was he there? Had he chosen that spot by accident, or was he trying to recapture the magic of the previous night that had vanished beneath the harsh reality of day?

She could recapture that magic all too easily: not just the passion and that final, shattering ecstasy, but the emotions that had filled the velvet darkness. Two people thrown together by merest chance had found something unexpected, something unique. She had come breathlessly close to telling him that she loved him, and those were words she'd never used before. Furthermore, she was certain that he too had felt the same way. They had been trembling on the very brink of something that would have changed their lives forever.

She remained still, watching him and feeling an awed sort of wonder that it should be this man in this place. Singing Waters had always been a magical place to her—a never-never land that remained forever unchanged and forever hers. She knew all its secrets and had often felt it calling to her while she went about her other life in Manhattan. But never once had she suspected that Singing Waters could yield up to her that one right man that she had secretly dreamed about.

That *did* seem uniquely appropriate, though. If she knew all

126

the secrets of this place, then perhaps it knew what lay hidden in her heart, too.

Annelise would never have described herself as a romantic. She'd always felt a secret scorn for such fuzzy-headed dreaming. Instead, she had gone about the task of building a life for herself that did not include a partner. But deep down inside, in that most hidden of places, a hope had remained. And on the day she'd opened the door to Max Armstrong, that hope had begun to quiver into life.

He was still staring off into the distance. She moved forward, staying behind the cover of the trees as she made her way around the end of the lake behind him. When she had reached his side of the lake, she checked to be certain that he hadn't spotted her, then sprinted for the rear of the house.

Max Armstrong was no romantic, either—or so he'd always believed. From time to time in his busy life, he'd met a woman who'd sparked a brief interest, but that interest had always died before it could flare up into anything serious.

He had his work and his hobbies and had always had a vague awareness that either or both of them could suffer if he should succumb to the lure of romance. There were those among his friends and colleagues who thought that Max was something of a playboy, and there had been women who had accused him of being afraid of making a commitment.

Since none of it was true, Max had largely ignored it. But still, he had wondered sometimes if he might be missing something in his life and would come to see that too late.

Now he *did* see it, and he refused to believe that it was too late. That knowledge had begun to build from the moment Annelise had appeared that first night for dinner, dispelling his earlier belief that she was just some freaky kid. And last night, here in the very spot where he now sat, he had finally known. She had, too.

The spark between them had exploded into brilliance. Max was confused about a lot of things right now, but there was one thing about which he was very sure: he didn't want that flame to be extinguished.

He continued to sit there, wondering when she would return from her walk and what she would do. He hadn't seen her since she'd left him in the library hours ago, but the housekeeper had told him that she'd gone for a walk.

Her solitary treks into the woods continued to bother him, but he now understood that there was little he could do to change matters. She needed her freedom and would probably always need it. He could possess her for moments or hours, but then she would take flight again, tantalizing him from that small but all-important distance.

Max never heard her come up behind him, and the first inkling he had of her presence was a rustling sound. He spun about quickly and saw sheets of yellow paper fluttering to the ground beside him.

She stood there in a faintly challenging stance, but the look in her eyes was one of uncertainty. Max glanced at the papers once more, realized what they were, then held out a hand to her.

She took it very gravely, stepping around the scattered papers to sit down beside him. Max continued to hold her hand, then lifted it slowly to his lips.

"Thank you," he said, knowing that she understood he was thanking her for far more than Otto's papers.

She nodded and he saw that the uncertainty remained in her eyes. She wrapped her arms about him and clung to him fiercely.

Max smiled, knowing how much it had cost her to give him the papers and what a significant gesture it was for her. So he held her and stroked her and kissed her softly, then felt her begin to tremble slightly with newly awakened desire.

His hand slid beneath the waistband of her shorts, and she shuddered still more, arching herself to him. Then suddenly, she stopped and pushed herself away from him as far as he would permit.

"We can't, Max. Mrs. M. and the girls . . ."

"I know that," Max said, although he had quite forgotten about them. "But they'll be gone soon."

But she drew away from him still more, then sat up. "I'm leaving, too."

"You're what?" Max scrambled into a sitting position as a chill shot through him.

She turned away from him to gather together the papers. "I'm going down to the city for a few days. The plane will be in Plattsburgh in less than two hours."

"What plane?" he asked, determined that she wouldn't be on it.

"Uncle Paul's jet," she explained. "Well, it actually belongs to one of the family's companies. I called for it before I left for my walk."

This time, Max totally ignored the evidence of her wealth. He was too worried about her imminent departure.

"I want you to stay here," he stated firmly.

She just smiled at him and held out the papers. "No, you don't. You want to see what Otto accomplished. And in any event, I *do* have to make a trip to Manhattan. I need to meet with the gallery owner about my show, and I also need to pick up some art supplies."

"If you can have steaks flown up here, you could have those supplies and the gallery owner flown up, too."

The smile remained as she shook her head. "I could, but I won't. You'll soon be so lost in those scribblings of Otto's that you won't even notice that I've gone."

"Not a chance," he stated, but his glance strayed briefly to the papers he now held.

She laughed and stood up, then bent to kiss the top of his head. "Those who demand space for themselves must also grant it to others, Max."

Manhattan seemed stifling, even though the worst of the summer had yet to descend upon the city. Annelise stepped out of the air-

129

conditioned coolness of the gallery into the heat and noise and glanced at her watch before sliding into the cool comfort of the limousine Paul had provided. She rarely opted for this form of transportation, but had given in to her uncle's insistence that this was the only way he could be reasonably certain she would arrive on time for their lunch date.

She sank into the deeply cushioned leather as the Rolls moved out into traffic. Now that her business with the gallery owner had been concluded, the uneasiness that had dogged her for the past day returned full force.

She had been the one who had requested this meeting with her uncle, but now she was uncertain about how to proceed. She knew she could always feign an interest in her financial affairs—something that never failed to please Paul—but that hadn't been the reason for this meeting.

She felt as though she were somehow betraying Otto by even telling Paul about the papers—and about Max's revelations. Certainly if it had been her father instead of Paul, she would have remained quiet. But Paul had always been close to Otto and had never disparaged his work. Besides, she supposed that as head of the family he had a right to know—especially if . . .

She forced that thought from her mind, just as she had done a hundred times already that day. Even last night, lying awake in bed, she had turned her thoughts to Otto largely to keep them away from Max. Thoughts of Otto working all those years in the library had dissolved into other childhood memories. Those memories had turned into full-fledged nightmares as she'd finally drifted off to sleep.

How much of all this she would tell Paul she didn't yet know, but she did know that what she really wanted from him was some sort of reassurance.

The Rolls glided to a stop before an elegant midtown building that was one of several owned by the family, and that housed the offices of several family concerns. The doorman greeted her and escorted her into the marble lobby, then pressed the button that opened Paul's private elevator.

Paul's secretary met her at the elevator and showed her into his private dining room, where a white-jacketed waiter quickly brought her a glass of wine. She settled into a gilded velvet chair and awaited her uncle's arrival.

She still hadn't decided just what she would tell him when he appeared, looking as aristocratic as always with his silvered hair and Savile Row suit. There had always been a strong resemblance between Paul and her father, she thought, but the difference became obvious when they smiled—as Paul did when he entered.

He bent to kiss her brow, then seated himself across from her and took the glass of wine proffered by the hovering waiter. "You're actually on time, Nellie. Does that mean this is serious business?"

She laughed to hide her nervousness. "No, it just means that the arrival of your chauffeur happened to coincide with the conclusion of my business."

"Is everything set for the show?"

"Everything but the paintings," she answered ruefully. "I've been somewhat distracted from my work."

"Oh? You mean that professor Hilde mentioned? Frankly, I'm surprised that you haven't tossed him out by now. I thought I detected a whiff of Hilde's matchmaking there. She told me that he's very attractive and implied that he's eminently suitable husband material."

She flushed at that, which drew a startled look from her uncle. "Good God, Nellie! Don't tell me that Hilde might have struck paydirt this time!"

"Um, well, that remains to be seen. But he *is* very interesting."

Paul laughed delightedly. "I must get up there to meet him. The thought of you with an academic type boggles the mind."

"Well, he isn't exactly typical," she protested. "And as a matter of fact, I think you'd like him very much."

"Wait until your mother hears about this." Paul grinned. "I'll

131

be seeing her when I go to London next week. She's coming over from Ireland for a few days."

"Don't get carried away, Paul. All I said was that Max is interesting."

They broke off then and Paul told the waiter to bring the first course of their lunch. Annelise found herself thinking about Max and her family. They *would* like him. But after all these years of noisy independence and even noisier complaints about family attempts at matchmaking, she found it difficult to accept that. The thought of them all smiling smugly did not sit well with her.

"So what does 'interesting' Max have to say about Otto's work?" Paul inquired after the waiter had departed.

"Well, that's what I wanted to talk to you about," she began.

Then she proceeded to tell Paul about the papers hidden in the painting and about Max's revelations. Paul listened in silence, but she could see his astonishment growing with every word. When she had finished, he got up to pour them both some more wine. He handed her glass to her and then reseated himself with a chuckle.

"Trust Otto to do the unexpected. You know, Nellie, I always did suspect that Otto truly was a genius, and it will please me as much as it must please you to see that proved. Have you talked with Armstrong since he's had these papers?"

She shook her head innocently, not bothering to mention how she had withheld the papers.

"No, but from what Max had seen of Otto's other work, he was pretty sure that Otto was on to something."

"I think you're absolutely correct in your assumption that Otto seized upon that man's disappearance to conceal his discovery. If Otto had any reason to believe that his discoveries could be used for other than peaceful purposes, he would never have made them public."

"But what do we do now?" she asked. "I mean, if Otto didn't want them to be made public, shouldn't we keep them private?"

"Well, it seems to me that question became moot when you gave them to Armstrong," Paul said.

"But I never told Max he could make them public."

"That doesn't matter. The point is that he now knows what they contain. He'd probably keep Otto's name out of it if we want it that way, but Otto's knowledge is now Armstrong's."

Annelise stared at him, dumbfounded. Somehow she had never considered that, but Paul was right. Max now knew what Otto had known, and he could take it from there. Their permission no longer mattered; knowledge couldn't be taken back. She couldn't believe that she had been so naïve.

The waiter returned with their lunch while she was still cursing her unbelievable stupidity. By the time he departed again, she was thinking uneasily that she might well have more problems with Max when she returned to Singing Waters. If Otto had had a good reason for not wanting this work published, then she intended to see that it wasn't published—with or without Otto's name.

"Paul, did Otto ever mention anything at all to you about this work?"

"Otto rarely mentioned his work to either your father or me, because neither of us understood it."

"I realize that, but I thought he might have spoken about it in a general sort of way. After all, this must have been very important to him if he lied about it and then hid it."

"But he did that work twenty years ago," Paul reminded her. Then he frowned thoughtfully. "Twenty years ago," he mused, staring off into space for a moment before focusing once more on his niece.

"You know, I *do* recall something that happened then, and I'm sure of the date because your grandmother died that following winter."

Annelise waited apprehensively as Paul tasted the chilled fruit soup and pronounced it excellent. She'd barely touched her own lunch.

"I have no way of knowing if what I remember had anything to do with this work, but both your father and I became somewhat concerned about Otto at that time. Neither of us had been able to spend much time up at Singing Waters that summer, so we both went up in the fall for Otto's birthday.

"Otto's behavior disturbed us both. He seemed nervous and, well, almost fearful. We both tried to find out what was bothering him, but he denied that anything was wrong. As I recall, we even talked to George about him, since George saw him every day and they were always close. But George insisted that Otto was fine and we finally dropped the matter.

"The next time we saw him, when he came to Bedford for Christmas, he seemed himself again. I can remember all this because we spent Christmas that year at Mother's, rather than at Singing Waters. She was already ill and couldn't make the trip. Then she died the following month."

Annelise vaguely remembered that Christmas—chiefly because of her grandmother's illness and the fact that the holidays had been spent at her Westchester estate rather than at Singing Waters. She could recall nothing about Otto's mood at the time, though; after all, she'd been only eight years old.

Paul went on in a thoughtful tone. "I suppose that the police questioning him about that man's disappearance, plus his decision to lie and withhold those papers, must have been troubling him. It *is* strange, though, that he didn't tell me about it. Otto and I were always closer than he and your father were."

Another typical Vandeveldt understatement, Annelise thought wryly. But far from finding the reassurance she had sought, she now felt an increasing uneasiness. Paul was probably right in his guess about what had been troubling Otto, but a nagging doubt remained in her mind.

She had little time to consider it, though, since the conversation turned to Paul's distress over the recent separation of his daughter from her husband. Annelise kept a prudent silence, since she didn't blame the husband at all. She couldn't stand her frivolous cousin. In point of fact, the husband had risen several notches in her opinion as a result of his having cried "Enough."

"Perhaps you've been wise not to have married yet, Nellie," Paul said when he had finished his discourse on the current family problem.

"I haven't really *planned* to remain single, Paul," she pointed out. "I'm just very particular, that's all."

"All the more reason why I should meet this Max Armstrong." Paul smiled. "I can't quite get a handle on the man, since both you and Hilde find him interesting. I would have thought that to be impossible."

At that moment, the man under discussion was relaxing after lunch on the small patio behind George's cottage. George's wife Mary had invited him to lunch after he had lavishly praised her pot roast the evening before. Max loved pot roast, but he hadn't quite had the nerve to suggest that Annelise serve it in the elegant dining room at Singing Waters. In fact, he rather doubted that she even knew what it was.

Max had discovered that George was a veritable encyclopedia of information about the Vandeveldts and about Singing Waters. He had been caretaker there for more than thirty years, and it appeared that very little had escaped his attention during that time.

Max had also learned that over the years George and Otto had become very close. Eventually theirs had become a true friendship rather than merely an employer-employee relationship.

He knew that he would be far better off forgetting about any possible secrets Singing Waters might hold, but he was still troubled by the too-timely disappearance of Harrington and Otto's lie about their work. However much he might later come to regret it, he felt compelled to make some effort to unravel that mystery.

He'd already told George about Otto's hidden papers and their importance—and now he tried to pursue the matter further. "So Otto never told you about those papers?" he asked.

135

George shook his gray head. "We never talked much about his work. He knew it was all Greek to me."

"Do you happen to recall the police coming here to question Otto about the disappearance of a professor named Harrington?" Max inquired, having deliberately withheld that information until now.

The two men were seated on chaises across from each other, and Max could plainly see the slight look of shock in George's eyes.

He knows something, Max thought uneasily, something he won't tell me.

"I was away when they came, but Otto mentioned it. He said he only knew the man slightly, that they'd worked on a few things together. Did that have something to do with the papers Nellie has found?"

Max then told George the whole story—including Otto's lie. As he did so, he watched George carefully, and there was just no mistaking his agitation.

"If Otto lied about the papers, he must have had a good reason," George said stoutly when Max had finished his story.

Max thought so, too, but he was beginning to suspect that it might not have been the altruistic reason Nellie had suggested.

Later, back at the house, Max sat behind the desk Otto had used and contemplated the recently discovered papers. It was brilliant work, as Harrington had apparently bragged.

Otto's theories, spread out on nine pages in his surprisingly small and neat hand, were unquestionably the work of genius and provided an enormous leap forward for Max in his own work. But still, it was rudimentary work, not the kind of thing he knew Annelise believed it to be. The world could neither be saved nor destroyed on the basis of these equations and hypotheses.

No, he was coming more and more to the unwelcome conclusion that Otto had hidden the papers primarily to cover his lie—a lie that was now beginning to make sense to Max.

In addition to the suspicions that George's nervousness had

aroused, there was the information gleaned quite unexpectedly from the housekeeper, who had begun working at Singing Waters twenty years ago as a maid.

The subject had arisen quite innocently as Max had been telling her about his travels. She had admitted to having done very little traveling, but then had gone on to say that the Vandeveldts were sending her and her husband to Hawaii in the fall as a twentieth anniversary present. As of this summer, she would have completed her twentieth year of service to Singing Waters and its owners.

With very little prodding from Max, she had gone on to describe that first summer, when, according to her, she had been so much in awe of the house and its owners that she hadn't done anything right.

She said that the Vandeveldts had all been very kind to her—even Nellie's father, who, she admitted, was a bit standoffish at times. Otto, she said, had been the kindest of them all—except at the end of the summer, when he'd begun to behave rather strangely. "Almost like he was afraid of something," she had mused. But then she had gone on to say that he'd gotten over it and become himself again.

The picture that she had painted of Otto was identical to the one he'd gotten from Annelise herself: a gentle, soft-spoken man whose behavior had belied his somewhat stern appearance. He was, the housekeeper had said, occasionally absentminded—but never mean.

Max had already seen several photos of Otto, including a portrait of him holding a six-year-old Annelise on his shoulders. He saw that photo now in his mind's eye and wondered how he could even be considering the possibility that such a man might have been capable of violence.

Annelise closed the gate behind her, then paused for a moment, shivering slightly in the early-evening chill. Up at the house, Max would be waiting, forewarned by the buzzer of her impending arrival.

For the first time in her life, she was nervous about returning to Singing Waters. The reassurances she'd sought from her meeting with Paul had been transformed into even greater concerns. And this brief absence from Max had served only to make her more unsure.

Paul's joking remark about the improbability of both she and Hilde liking Max bothered her far more than it should have. That rebelliousness against her family that seemed to have been born with her was surfacing once more. How on earth could she possibly be interested in a man who met with her aunt's approval?

Perhaps Max wasn't all she had believed him to be. He *was* very attractive, and they had been thrust together in this beautiful, isolated place she loved so much. Under such circumstances, her judgment might well be suspect.

Such were her thoughts as she got back into the Porsche and roared off up the long drive to Singing Waters, taking comfort in the beauty of the familiar surroundings but fearful of what awaited her.

Dusk was just settling in around the big house when she first saw it, and for a moment she failed to notice the tall figure sitting on the edge of the fountain. But then he stood up, and a small, involuntary sound escaped from her lips as she caught sight of him.

Once more, she was struck by the rightness of it all—of Max and Singing Waters. She'd always felt an embarrassing possessiveness toward this place—and now she felt that possessiveness extend itself to the man who stood waiting for her. That thought was very frightening to a woman who had always fought any attempts on the part of others to possess her.

Instead of driving on to the garage, she pulled up in the circular drive around the fountain. Max had her door open even before the car's engine had died. Before she could get out, he reached in and scooped her up into his arms, then stifled her greeting with a

138

fierce and demanding kiss. To her even greater astonishment, she responded in kind, seeking his mouth hungrily and meeting the erotic thrust of his tongue with her own.

Then the fierceness was gone and Max was grinning at her. "If that had been a poacher instead of you, he'd have been in big trouble."

"He certainly would have—if you'd greeted him like this," she rejoined somewhat self-consciously.

He continued to cradle her in his arms as he devoured her with his eyes. "I've missed you," he said huskily.

"Then Otto's papers must not be as interesting as we'd thought," she replied, unwilling as yet to admit even to herself just how much she had missed him.

"They were very interesting, but for some strange reason, I find *you* even more interesting."

"Are you trying to avoid the subject, Max?" she asked archly.

"No, I'm trying to *change* the subject—but since you won't let me, I will tell you this: Otto has not discovered a new way to destroy mankind."

"Are you sure?" she persisted even in her relief at his words.

"Yes, I'm sure," he replied in a tone meant to end the discussion.

"But what *did* he discover?"

Max started determinedly toward the house, ignoring her struggles to be set down, and also ignoring her continued questions.

She had fully expected him to carry her on up the stairs, but to her surprise, he headed for the library. At first, she thought that her questions might be precipitating a lesson in physics that she didn't really want right now, but when he stopped in the doorway, she let out a cry of surprise.

"Well, what do you think?" he asked with a grin. "Other than the Jacuzzi, this place doesn't really offer much in the way of sensuality, so I did the best I could."

She laughed nervously as she felt a languorous heat burn away at her reason. He had apparently raided the linen closets to come up with a huge down comforter and some pillows, then moved the leather sofa to make room for them in front of the fireplace, where flames crackled brightly, creating the only light in the room. Two snifters of cognac rested on a silver tray nearby.

"I think you did rather well," she said breathlessly. "How did you manage all this in the time it took me to drive up from the gate?"

"Careful advance planning," he responded smugly. "Of course, the effect wouldn't have been quite the same if you'd arrived during the day."

They smiled at each other, feeling silly and embarrassed and pleased: two determinedly unromantic people caught in the world's oldest trap. He carried her to the fireplace and set her down on the soft comforter.

"I just need a few more minutes to complete the scene," he said as he knelt beside her and began to unbutton her blouse.

So she let him undress her, which he did with tantalizing slowness, pausing frequently to caress the creamy flesh he had exposed. When he had finished, he stood up and stared at her with an intensity that washed over her like waves of desire.

Max felt a flood tide of need coursing through him as he looked at her, small and sleek and vulnerably naked in the middle of the comforter.

His fingers shook as he tore off his own clothing far more rapidly, baring himself to her gaze and seeing in her eyes a powerful reflection of his own all-consuming need. Supremely conscious of his every movement, he knelt beside her.

The light of the fire bathed her in a flickering, ruddy glow, creating a portrait of such stunning eroticism that Max's breath caught in his throat. For long moments, he didn't even touch her as he filled his eyes with her delicate beauty. She reached out a hand to him, and he seized it and carried it to his lips. Then, after kissing her cupped palm, he trailed his lips and tongue slowly along the length of her outstretched arm.

Max had had every intention of taking it slowly, of savoring each and every moment—but from the instant he touched her and felt her quivering response, he forgot all about those intentions.

He circled one dark nipple and immediately felt it harden. He trailed his fingers down along her warm, soft body and heard her moan as he reached the molten core of her womanhood. As his mouth followed his hands, she arched to him and reached for him, setting off tremors along his entire body as she caressed him intimately.

Then, when he had filled all his senses completely with her, Max poured himself into her and hoarsely whispered his love into the explosion that followed.

CHAPTER NINE

The problem of Otto and the vanished Professor Harrington did not go away, as they both privately wished that it would. Instead, they allowed it to be buried in the dark recesses of their minds where it lurked, quiescent now but still there.

It was very easy to ignore a problem so distant in time, because love's floodgates had opened for them both on the night of her return. In the stillness after passion's fury had been spent, Max had repeated his declaration of love, and Annelise had used those precious words for the first time.

Each day took on a splendor of its own. Max worked, Annelise painted—and they both accomplished a great deal, somewhat to their surprise. Love was a force that filled their lives, touching everything they did, and its unique energy flowed onto canvas and paper.

When she asked him about the newly discovered papers, Max was carefully vague, saying only that he needed more time to digest the information they contained. She let it go at that, only too happy to avoid the confrontation she had feared.

She invited him to join her on her daily treks into the woods and Max required no further urging. They roamed the forests and fields of Singing Waters and made love several times in leafy green bowers, feeling wanton and primitive and very happy.

Hilde called, proving that the family grapevine was in good working order. After chatting about inconsequential matters for several minutes, she finally got down to the business of determining just how successful her matchmaking had been. She obviously considered this to be her doing. Mellowed by love, Annelise was disinclined to contradict her aunt.

Her mother called from Ireland, where she was spending the summer with relatives. She'd just returned from London, where Paul had filled her in. She was full of questions about this man who seemed to have captivated her daughter, and was every bit as astonished as Paul had been.

"Well, he's a sort of Indiana Jones type, Mum," Annelise explained. "Not the usual academic type at all."

"Now I think I'm beginning to understand," her mother replied. "But I'm sure that I'll soon have a more objective report from Paul."

So Annelise was more or less prepared for the next call. Paul suggested casually that he might enjoy a weekend's fishing at Singing Waters if his presence wouldn't be unwelcome. Annelise felt certain that Paul hadn't done any fishing for years, but she didn't point that out as she invited him to come up.

"Prepare yourself, Max," she stated when she told him about her uncle's planned visit. "Paul takes his role as head of the family *very* seriously."

The following Friday afternoon, they were both lying naked on the raft in the middle of the lake, having given up swimwear except when the staff were present. The sun's heat had just succeeded in thawing their temporarily frozen desire when Annelise heard a droning sound in the distance and sat up, shading her eyes as she scanned the heavens.

"That's probably Paul," she stated as the sound grew louder and became recognizable as a jet engine.

Max sat up, too, and the two of them watched as the sleek white jet dipped a wing and circled low over Singing Waters before climbing once more into the heavens and accelerating off toward the northeast. Annelise laughed at Max's mortified expression.

"If he'd come a few minutes later, he would really have gotten an eyeful," she said, grinning wickedly.

If Max was nervous about meeting the head of the Vandeveldt family, it didn't show when Paul arrived a little over an hour later, driving the old Volvo wagon the family kept at the airport. Unlike Annelise's father, whose cool propriety had rarely thawed, Paul was capable of a relaxed sort of charm, especially here in this place he loved.

"I shouldn't be surprised to find pieces of aircraft raining down on the lake," Paul stated dryly. "Midair collisions could become quite a problem if you two keep forgetting your bathing suits."

"We'll keep that in mind," Annelise answered in the same tone, while Max looked chagrined.

The two men hit it off well and went fishing together the next morning, although Annelise suspected that catching their dinner was far from the primary purpose of the expedition. They did, however, return with two very large bass that had somehow been overlooked by the loons. The flavorful fish were grilled by Annelise for dinner and enjoyed by all.

They bade good-bye to Paul the next afternoon, then linked arms and started back toward the house.

"Well, what did you two talk about all that time out on the lake?" Annelise asked curiously.

"Oh, this and that," Max said with elaborate casualness. "Phrases like 'occasionally difficult' and 'something of a problem' kept cropping up in the conversation. I had the sense that I was being warned about something."

"Warned?" she asked incredulously. "Is that why he came up here?"

Max laughed and swept her into his arms. "I think he came to see if I'm up to the task."

She didn't bother asking anything more.

Max felt a guilty sort of pleasure as he stood beside Annelise, watching the sleek jet sweep in for a landing. Behind him, he heard the appreciative sounds of several teenagers as they too spotted the plane. He could easily identify with them. As a kid, he too had loved planes and flying. Several times over the years, he had considered getting his pilot's license, but had always decided against it. Getting the license would have been no problem, but flying was a very expensive hobby, and Max already had too many expensive hobbies.

He glanced down at Annelise, then quickly looked away again. He was remembering that conversation where she had stated that the Vandeveldt money had enabled Hilde's husband Rowan to pursue all his hobbies. It was true. Rowan Newcombe owned a very expensive racing yacht that he could never have afforded on his academic salary.

Max wondered how Rowan had managed it. Did he ever suffer any doubts about himself as a result of enjoying his wife's largess? Perhaps Rowan had come to terms with it long before Max had met him.

Max prided himself on being a modern, non-sexist male, but down inside, he still believed that men were intended to be the breadwinners.

Annelise had summoned the jet once more, this time to take them to Boston for a few days. Max had told her that he wanted to return to MIT to pick up a computer console that would hook him up by phone to the MIT computers, an indispensable aid in analyzing parts of Otto's work. He also wanted to discuss the work with his department head.

He'd fully expected her to accept his absence, since she was deeply engrossed in her painting, but to his surprise and pleasure, she had immediately suggested going with him. Since Max had no idea when her need for freedom might reassert itself, he thought it best to take advantage of the time he had. Besides, he hadn't really wanted to be away from her for even a few days.

Then, when he'd announced his intention to drive back to Boston, she had suggested they use the plane if it was available. Max had almost said no, but when he searched his mind for a reason to refuse, he found none that she would never accept. So here they were.

A short while later, they were airborne, seated across from each other in the low, cushioned seats with Max's long legs extending into the narrow aisle. He'd been surprised at the cramped interior space, since the graceful plane gave the impression of being quite large. He said as much to her.

"Oh, there *is* a larger plane. I forget what it is, but it has desks and even a small galley and bedroom. But for short flights this is okay."

Max groaned inwardly. Competition for Air Force One, no doubt. "How many other planes are there in the Vandeveldt air force?"

"That's it." She smiled. "Except for the helicopter that Paul uses to commute from his home in Connecticut to Manhattan."

Then she looked at him levelly. "This bothers you, doesn't it?"

Max hesitated, then nodded somewhat sheepishly.

"You're being very old-fashioned, Max. You certainly wouldn't expect me to be bothered if the situation were reversed."

He nodded again, wishing that she'd change the subject.

"Well, at some point, you're just going to have to come to terms with it."

"Am I?" he asked with a trace of a smile.

"Don't play games, Max. It won't do either of us any good for you to pretend that my money doesn't exist."

Max had almost forgotten just how outspoken she could sometimes be. But he knew she was right.

"I haven't been avoiding the issue," he protested, although he knew that he had. "It just hasn't *been* an issue up to this point."

"It's nothing more than an accident of birth, you know. If I were forced to rely on my own resources to live, I'd probably be waitressing somewhere or playing the starving artist for real."

Max was stunned to realize that she meant it. He'd quite forgotten that day when she had hinted at insecurities about her art.

146

Most of the time, she projected an image of total self-assurance that left no room for doubts.

"I find that difficult to believe," he said, for lack of anything better to say.

"But it's true," she insisted. "Technically, I'm unemployed right now. Art is a profession only if one sells one's work."

"But you *have* sold your work?"

"Of course, but not for any great sums. Not long ago—just after I signed the contract for this show—I sat down and calculated my earnings to date and decided that I would have starved to death about three years ago. And that was allowing for only a very modest standard of living."

Max was going to protest that it hardly mattered, since she could live any way she chose—with or without the sale of her paintings. But he kept quiet, because he knew it *did* matter—to her, at least.

Her very determined independence and occasional attempts to distance herself from her illustrious family now began to make a lot more sense to Max. She wasn't content to be just a Vandeveldt, or even the Vandeveldt who paints. She wanted and needed her own identity, and her money was perhaps an even greater obstacle to her than it was to him.

He reached across the aisle and took her hand in his, then brought it to his lips. In this manner, with these small admissions, and through this kind of understanding, his love grew still more.

She saw that love in his eyes, then quickly lowered her gaze. At times like this, she felt frighteningly vulnerable. She knew instinctively that he understood—but she wasn't completely certain that she truly wanted his understanding.

They landed at Logan Airport after being stacked up for nearly half an hour, then took a cab to Max's Cambridge apartment.

The graduate student to whom Max had sublet his home for the summer was there, and Max was relieved to see that he hadn't destroyed the place. It was a large, sunny apartment that Max had bought as soon as the building had gone co-op a few years ago. He'd furnished it in a very modern style, but over the years had picked up a few antiques that had appealed to him, as well as some paintings that Annelise now examined closely.

Max divided his time between watching her and smiling inwardly at the goggling graduate student whose eyes hadn't left her since their arrival. It was obvious that both the woman and her name had made a big impression on the young man.

"Well?" he asked when she finally turned around.

"Exactly the sort of thing I would have expected you to have," she said with a noncommittal shrug.

"Oh?" He didn't know what to make of that.

"Strongly suggestive of Mondrian. Very geometric. Exactly what I'd expect a scientist to like."

"You don't like them," Max stated, feeling rather disappointed.

"I didn't say that. They just aren't my style. But the quality is certainly good enough."

"Are you an artist, Ms. Vandeveldt?" The student asked in a tone that suggested that being a Vandeveldt must surely be enough.

"Perhaps," she replied with a smile that was directed at Max. "That remains to be seen."

Max lounged in a beach chair, engaged in a conversation with their host that would have been incomprehensible to most people. But since their host was also Max's department chairman, the subject was understandable—to them, at least.

"Umm, back up a bit there, Max. I think you've gotten sidetracked." The older man regarded his protégé with fond amusement. "Or maybe 'distracted' would be a better word."

Max chuckled and gave up his attempt to keep his eyes off Annelise. She was farther down the beach, clad in a black and white swimsuit that matched her striking hair, which was piled in a loose knot atop her head. She was also surrounded by their host's three grandchildren, whom she had already taken to referring to as the "Munchkins."

The children's cries suggested that she must be drawing their portraits as she sat on the wet, packed sand with a large sketchpad and a charcoal pencil. Max recalled that she had said once she didn't like to do portraits, and he suspected that three active children weren't exactly her cup of tea, either.

Still, despite all this, the children were quite obviously drawn to her and had been following her around ever since she'd arrived at this beachfront house on Cape Cod. Annelise apparently had the capacity to draw people of all ages to her—or rather, to have them following along in her wake.

When Max had contacted Professor Penberthy, his department head, they had promptly received an invitation to spend the day with him and Annelise had readily agreed, so long as Max didn't insist that they also visit Hilde, who was at her home in Hyannis. Max was actually hoping that she might change her mind about that, since he had a wicked desire to see Annelise in action against her formidable aunt.

The two men stretched their considerable brain power a while longer, then turned to a consideration of the other problem presented by the discovery of Otto's papers.

"It doesn't sound good, does it?" Professor Penberthy said when Max had finished his story. "Still, from what you've told me about him, it's hard to believe that Vandeveldt could have had anything to do with Harrington's disappearance."

"That's exactly how I feel," Max concurred. "But I'm sure that the caretaker knows more than he's telling. If you'd seen him, you'd agree."

"Even the timing is right," Max went on. "Harrington disappeared just before Labor Day, and the housekeeper said that Otto's behavior changed around that time."

"But Harrington's car was found in Manhattan—quite a distance."

"True—but what better place to dump a car? And as you said,

149

no one knew of any reason why Harrington should have gone to New York."

Penberthy looked down the beach, then back at Max. "Does she know anything, do you think?"

"No, I'm sure she doesn't. She would have been just a kid then, don't forget."

"Yes, but kids have a way of noticing things that can escape an adult's attention, and you said that she was very close to her uncle."

Max nodded. "She always spent her summers there, too. If anything did happen at Singing Waters, she might well have been there at the time."

Max looked again at Annelise, who turned just then and gave him a rueful shrug before returning to her sketching.

"Otto was like a father to her," he told the other man. "She idolized him."

"Well, the police closed that case long ago, so there's no need for you to pursue it, Max."

Max nodded. He'd been telling himself just that for weeks now.

"But you will pursue it, won't you?" Penberthy said gently. He had come to know Max very well and realized Max was possessed of that insatiable curiosity that is the hallmark of all great scientists—an exalted status the older man was confident Max would one day attain. He knew also that Max had a keen sense of justice that, in this particular case, could easily lead him into personal disaster. It didn't take much perception to see that Max was very much in love.

Max was fully aware of these potentially dangerous qualities. To try to pursue this matter could only lead to serious problems. And yet the need to know gnawed at him in exactly the way the need to understand the complexities of physics drove him. That same unquenchable need had led him into danger in his hobbies as well. The mountain was there, so it had to be climbed. The cave existed; therefore, it must be explored.

His sense of justice in this particular case was somewhat more murky. If anything had happened, it had happened a long time ago, and it was five years too late for Otto to be brought to justice if he had actually done anything wrong. What he sought was more in the realm of personal knowledge. *He* had to know; whether anyone else needed to know was still open to question. Certainly, he had no desire to see Annelise's memories of her beloved uncle tainted.

As Max sat there thinking about all this, Annelise and the children descended upon them. After they had duly admired the sketches, Max and their host were dragged into a game of Frisbee with the children, while Annelise took over his chair and continued her sketching.

Later, when the children had gone up to the house with their grandfather, Max returned to find her dozing in the late-afternoon sun, her sketchpad cast aside. He picked it up and was startled to see his own likeness staring back at him.

"That's not bad," he said when she woke up.

She held it up and peered at it critically. "It still needs some work."

Max stretched and looked down at his swimsuit-clad body. "Maybe you should do a complete nude," he suggested jokingly.

She looked him up and down with a smile. "I've been thinking about that. I always did like to sketch male nudes. Men have such interesting bodies."

Max bent to kiss her lightly. "I doubt that you've ever known a male body as well as you know this one."

"That's very true," she remarked, thinking that he just might regret his suggestion one day.

He stifled a yawn. "It's been a long day. I really think you should call Hilde and have her put us up for the night."

"There are plenty of other places we could stay," she replied.

"And you don't want to give Hilde the satisfaction of knowing that her matchmaking has succeeded," he finished for her.

But he won in the end. They stayed for dinner with the

Penberthys, then left for Rowan and Hilde's after Annelise had called her aunt.

Max found the evening to be highly amusing. As he'd suspected, Annelise and Hilde were very well matched. Both women had mastered the art of understatement and possessed considerable talent for clothing scathing remarks in complimentary attire.

Max himself contributed to the proceedings by seizing every possible opportunity to demonstrate that he and Annelise were far more than the friends she was portraying them to be. He ignored both the discreet distance she tried to maintain and her angry looks.

Finally, when aunt and niece began to dissect the broken marriage of Paul's daughter—naturally taking opposing points of view—Rowan got up and suggested that he and Max step outside for some air. Max was enjoying the discussion, but could scarcely decline Rowan's invitation.

As soon as they were out on the terrace, Rowan lit his pipe and cast a glance back over his shoulder with a chuckle.

"I thought you might have had enough."

"Actually," Max said with a grin, "I've found it very interesting. They're well matched."

Rowan nodded, still chuckling. "Nellie might have been much better off if we'd had a daughter, instead of sons. I understand that you've now met Paul, too."

"Yes, and to tell you the truth I liked him."

"I do, too. It's probably just as well, though, that you won't have to meet John. That was Nellie's father."

"They didn't get along very well, did they—Nellie and her father, I mean?"

Rowan drew thoughtfully on his pipe. "John loved Nellie, although I don't think anyone will ever be able to convince her of that. And perhaps in some ways, the situation was exacerbated by the fact that Otto took a shine to Nellie from the day she was born."

Max hadn't really intended to seek any information about Otto from Rowan, simply because it hadn't occurred to him to do so, but since the opportunity had presented itself, he decided to take advantage of it.

"Yes, I know they were very close. He seems to have been an interesting man."

Rowan smiled through a cloud of tobacco smoke. "There's no such thing as a *dull* Vandeveldt, believe me. But Otto was certainly the most fascinating of his generation—just as Nellie is of hers. It's no wonder the two were so close.

"Otto and I got along well from the beginning, but in all the years I knew him, I never quite figured him out. He was a brilliant man, as you now know, but he often seemed insecure about his genius. He wasn't a hermit type, by any means, and yet he lived like one. You could get close to him, but then you'd discover that something was still eluding you."

Max thought that that description sounded uncannily like Annelise. "I can't figure out why he would have hidden those papers. Does it make any sense to you?"

"I've been thinking about that. We never really talked much about his work. But something about the timing bothers me. I could be off base, but I don't think so." He paused, then resumed.

"Yes, I'm pretty sure I'm right, because it was that next winter that Hilde's mother died, and she mentioned just recently that that was nearly twenty years ago.

"Anyway, what I was going to say is that Otto started to act a little strange around that period. John and Paul were both worried about him, although George, the caretaker, told them nothing was wrong."

"What do you mean by 'a little strange'?" Max inquired.

"Well, we got this secondhand from John and Paul, but it was enough to send Hilde scurrying up there to see for herself. She stayed for a few days and then came back worried, too.

"She said he seemed nervous and distracted, and that he'd been doing some strange things. The housekeeper—that was the one before Mrs. Mayhew—had told her something about Otto doing some repair work—cement work, I think. I really can't recall exactly what it was, but it didn't sound like Otto. The man had no talent for that sort of thing, and besides, there were others to do work like that.

"We all kept in close touch with him through the rest of that fall, but by Christmastime, he seemed to be fine again. I'm not sure how that could have had anything to do with his decision to lie about that work, but like I said, the timing seems right."

Max felt a cold, hard lump in the pit of his stomach. He tried to tell himself that he was doing some Olympic-class jumping to conclusions, but the feeling wouldn't go away.

"I imagine that you must be feeling a little overwhelmed at this point, Max."

It took Max a few seconds to realize that Rowan had changed the subject and was obviously referring to Annelise. He nodded, grateful for the switch.

"Well, then, take some advice from one who's been there. I know you come from pretty much the same background as I do, and I think I know just how you feel. But the money is unimportant, Max. It's unimportant to them, and it should be just as unimportant to you."

"Unimportant?" Max said incredulously. "How can all those millions be unimportant?"

"It's hundreds of millions, actually," Rowan said dryly, "and it's unimportant to them because they've had it for so long. John was the only one who ever cared about money, and for him, it was just the challenge of making more.

"I've learned something over the years from association with the family and others in their circle. Money only seems to matter to those who don't have it or those who haven't had it for very long. For people like the Vandeveldts, it has about the same degree of importance as the air they breathe or the water they drink."

Max nodded slowly. What Rowan said made sense, he supposed—even if Max, as an outsider, still found it incomprehensible.

"And they're not snobs," Rowan went on. "I know that they can seem that way to people when they first meet them, but it isn't snobbery. Every one of them has at some time had people try to use them, and for that reason there's a certain reticence, a holding back. It's a defense mechanism and nothing more. Usually people are snobs because they're insecure, unsure of their place in society. But there's no need for that when you're at the very top."

Max nodded again, then turned to look back into the living room, where Hilde and Annelise were still engaged in animated conversation. Rowan was right, but Max sensed that with that security came a unique form of vulnerability, too. They lived in a gilded cage, to be sure—but there were still bars, and they knew it.

From the beginning he'd been drawn to that fascinating, unique combination of strength and vulnerability in Annelise.

The men rejoined the women then, interrupting a spirited discussion about art, and shortly thereafter, Rowan and Hilde excused themselves, saying it was getting late. Max wrapped an arm about Annelise, ignoring her attempt to move away, and suggested that they go for a walk on the beach before turning in.

As soon as they were out of the house, he remarked casually that it was thoughtful of Hilde to have provided them with adjoining rooms.

"That's exactly how we're going to spend the night, too—in adjoining rooms," she stated firmly. "Your behavior was inexcusable, Max. Hilde is probably planning the wedding right now."

Max smiled at the way she cut off the sentence abruptly, as though she'd spoken without thought and had suddenly realized it halfway through.

Then Max wondered just when it was that he had realized he was going to spend the rest of his life with her. Marriage hadn't been discussed; in fact, no mention of the future had been made by either of them. But he knew instinctively that she felt just as he did. However, he also knew that this was not the best time to tell her that.

"I didn't do or say anything that wasn't true," he protested.

"No, but no one could accuse you of being discreet, either." She scowled at him, then abruptly burst out laughing.

"Hilde will probably spend the rest of her life claiming that *she* was the one who brought us together. But it was really Otto." She paused for an instant, then went on.

"What did Professor Penberthy have to say about Otto's work?"

Max hesitated. He knew it would be easy to lie or to be non-committal, but he suspected the truth would have to come out sooner or later.

"He agrees with my assessment."

"Which is what? You've been awfully vague about it, Max."

"I can't help being vague," Max replied. "If you were a physicist, then I could be specific. Otto's work is fascinating and very original. It should be published. But it will be years before we know just how important it is. What he's provided amounts to a signpost, pointing in a given direction. But until we actually get there, we can't know if it's the *right* direction."

She sat down at the edge of a dune and looked up at him. "I don't understand, Max. If what you're saying is true, then Otto wasn't worried about his work having dire consequences. Why would Otto have concealed the work?"

Max dropped down beside her. "I don't know," he said. Only he could have answered that.

"Well, maybe if it *is* published, someone else will see something you've missed."

"That's always possible, but Penberthy is the acknowledged expert in that area, and I'm considered to be something of an expert myself."

She drew up her knees and rested her chin on them thoughtfully. "He *had* to have had a reason for doing such a thing. After all, all his other papers were right there in plain view."

Then she turned to look at him. "And there's also the fact that he lied about their existence. Wasn't Penberthy the one who talked to him about it?"

Max nodded.

She turned away again, her expression pensive as she stared out at the darkened ocean. "Max," she began in a strangely childlike tone. Then she stopped abruptly and resumed a more normal voice.

"Well, there's no point trying to speculate about it. It's over and done with."

Max doubted that it was over, and for the first time he sensed that she too doubted it. He knew that if she had any suspicions at all, she would pursue them for all she was worth, regardless of where they might lead and regardless of how badly the truth could hurt her.

"You're right. Let's discuss something far more important and immediate—like our sleeping arrangements for tonight." He slid his arms about her and drew her to him.

She continued to insist upon separate rooms right up to the moment Max joined her in her bed. But Annelise's determination was no match for Max's, and he knew exactly how to change her mind. He proceeded to demonstrate that knowledge very thoroughly.

So Max spent the night exactly where he had wanted to spend it, and in the morning, Annelise went into the unused bedroom and rumpled the bed.

Hilde was not fooled when the lovers appeared late for breakfast the next morning.

CHAPTER TEN

Annelise awoke to a brilliant flash of lightning. The echoes of the thunder that had awakened her reverberated through Singing Waters. There was a strange moment of confusion when she actually thought of herself as a child, frightened once more by a ferocious storm.

She sat up in bed and that strange impression slowly died. But as childhood ebbed away into memory, an awareness of the bed's emptiness took its place.

Where was Max? She looked around the darkened room just as another sharp crack of thunder was followed a split-second later by an even more brilliant flash of lightning that outlined the windows and poured through the partially opened drapes. There was no movement from the heavy drapes, so she knew he must have closed the windows.

She got slowly out of bed and grabbed her long ivory silk robe from a nearby chair and slipped it over her naked body. Apparently the storm had awakened Max before it had roused her and he had left the room to avoid disturbing her. But his absence *did* disturb her now.

More thunder crashed around the big house, actually rattling the heavy, leaded windows before subsiding into a drawn-out series of low growls that sounded almost as though a living creature were lurking out there in the darkness. Annelise recalled that she had once believed just that.

In the flash of lightning that accompanied the growl, she saw that Max's pants were missing from the other chair, although his light sweater remained. The vague reassurance that sweater gave her brought a smile to her face.

She picked up the sweater, then buried her face in it for a moment before she began to feel distinctly foolish and dropped it again. But his scent lingered, teasing her and stirring up that mixture of remembered and anticipated desire that trembled through her and made the cool silk of her robe feel like ice against her suddenly heated body.

Then she went to one of the windows and stared out at the black night as more thunder rumbled and a bolt of forked lightning arced in the heavens before dipping low, probably to claim some tall tree on the hill behind the house. After its light had waned, she noticed the pale splash of light that spilled across the terrace and realized that Max must be in the library.

As she walked down the carpeted hallway, more thunder shook the house, and the crystal wall sconces tinkled musically and dimmed, then came back again. For one more brief moment, that child in her reawakened, brought back by the storm and the darkness and the silence within the house. She actually paused for a moment outside the room that had been her parents' before shaking herself mentally and hurrying on down the staircase.

Max had his back to her as he stood at the french doors, staring out at the storm. She paused there, content for the moment now that she had reassured herself of his presence. His wavy brown hair was still tousled from sleep and stuck out at odd angles. He was shirtless and shoeless and his close-fitting jeans emphasized his lean, hard body. Annelise thought again of his teasing remark about painting him in the nude and vowed that she would do just that. He was right; she knew his body well enough to paint it from memory.

She shivered lightly, not from the temperature, but from the awakened need that washed over her, a need for closeness more than for passion. It was this strange, new need that confused and frightened her—but Max seemed to understand it well. Despite her complaints about his openly affectionate behavior before Hilde, Annelise found that she wanted and needed that closeness now.

Perhaps that need somehow communicated itself to him, because he turned his head slightly, then spun about when he saw her there. She went to him wordlessly, and he immediately wrapped his arms about her, rumpling the silken barrier between them.

"I couldn't sleep and I didn't want to disturb you," he said as he pressed his mouth against the top of her head. "This is a first-rate storm."

"They're always so violent up here," she agreed. "Or maybe it's just that I never notice them much in Manhattan."

Max continued to hold her as they watched the storm's pyrotechnics. Ever since their return from Boston two days earlier, he'd been trying to decide what to do.

If Rowan's memory had been accurate—and Max believed that it was, Singing Waters might well hold an ugly secret, one it had held silently for nearly twenty years. Still, it was hard to believe such a thing, and Max didn't want to believe it.

Standing here earlier, he had decided that he would nose around the house a bit more, keeping in mind Rowan's comment about cement work and if he found nothing, he was going to force his ugly suspicions from his mind. But if he *did* find something . . .

The room was suddenly plunged into a blackness so total that all Max could see in those first few seconds were the white streak in her hair as she nestled more tightly against his chest, and the long white robe that shimmered beneath his fingers.

"I believe that you mentioned a generator at some point," he said when the power remained out.

"Yes, it's in a room in the garage."

"We may need it. This is what the weather people call 'dangerous lightning,' the kind that goes air to ground instead of just air to air. So the lines could be down."

"That seems to be the only kind of storm we get up here," she said ruefully. "Between that and the winter storms, the generator gets a lot of use. Otto had it put in years ago. George will—" She stopped. "That's right. George and Mary are away."

"Don't you know how to start it?" he asked half-teasingly.

"I have a negative mechanical aptitude," she stated with perverse pride. "Besides, I hate the thing. It's ugly and noisy."

"You *do* have this thing against noise and ugliness." He grinned, recalling her comments about his dirt bike.

"I'm an artist. We prefer to dwell in beauty and silence."

"And in this case, darkness," Max finished for her. "Do you happen to know where there's a flashlight downstairs?"

"In the kitchen. But I always rather fancied myself wandering about with a lighted candelabra in hand. That's far more aesthetically pleasing than a flashlight, and we have some lovely candelabra."

Max let her go with a chuckle and started for the door. "Well, you go play Lady MacBeth if you want. I'm going to get the flashlight and go deal with the generator."

She turned around and her gaze fell on the bookcase that concealed the staircase—just as it was starkly illuminated by another flash of lightning. That childhood memory erupted again, leaving in its wake a trail of icy fear.

"I'm going with you," she said, hurrying to catch up to him in the darkness.

He wrapped an arm about her waist as they walked toward the kitchen. "Don't tell me that you're afraid of storms."

"I was once," she replied, and tried to bury that memory once more.

Max peered into the dark corners of the basement, while keeping his ears tuned for any sound that might indicate that Annelise had come to find him. He'd already taken the precaution of setting up the billiards table to cover his presence here.

Such skulking about did not come naturally to Max, and he felt guilty as hell. But at the moment, curiosity outweighed guilt. Right now, it was a challenge, a game, but he knew that if he should actually find anything, the game would become serious business indeed. More serious than he cared to contemplate.

First, he conducted a search of the boiler room. It was farthest from the stairs and even the noise of the small burner that heated the hot water would have masked her arrival. But he reasoned that she was unlikely to come after him this quickly.

Then he opened doors and peered into two storage rooms, which were completely empty and therefore quite easy to check. There was no sign anywhere of the cement work Rowan had mentioned and Max knew that not even a skilled craftsman could have completely hidden all traces of such work. From what Rowan had said about Otto's abilities as a handyman, Max guessed that his work would be readily identifiable.

He walked back along the hallway, then opened the door into yet another storage room, this one lined on three walls with rows of ancient shelving. The fourth wall had a door in its center, a very old door that looked quite heavy.

Max approached it with what he knew was excessive caution, and saw immediately that it hadn't been opened in a long time. His mental map of the basement told him that there should be a fairly sizable room there, however.

He grasped the metal doorknob and pulled, afraid of what he might find. The door creaked open with a metallic groan that he was sure could be heard throughout the house. Unnaturally cold air rushed out at him, carrying with it a distinctly fetid smell combined with a damp earthiness. He backed away slightly, wrinkling his nose at the odor even as he tried to identify it.

He pulled out his small pocket flashlight and flicked it on, aiming it into the room. As the narrow beam pierced the darkness, Max realized the purpose of the room and the source of the smell and very nearly sagged with relief.

He'd never actually seen a root cellar before, but he was sure that this was what it had been. The heavy oak door and the earthen floor and walls would have provided a natural refrigerator for Singing Waters during the early years of its existence. Although nothing was left of the food once stored in there, the ancient smell of produce still lingered.

He played the narrow beam over the entire room and saw nothing more than some tiny, scurrying shapes that had obviously been shocked into action by the intrusion.

He pushed the door shut again, once more aware of the loud groan of protesting hinges, then realized that the room in which he stood must once have been a well-stocked larder, with shelves groaning from the weight of preserved foods. At a time when the entire family, plus servants and guests, had spent their summers here, the place would probably have rivaled any modern supermarket.

He started back to the billiards room, then paused outside the wine cellar. He'd already been in there several times, but all that had been before he'd had any reason to pay much attention to the place.

The room was fairly well lit by overhead bulbs, and Max walked around it slowly, peering into spaces between the rows of bottles in their specially built racks. He saw that some repointing had been done in places to the ancient brick wall, but he'd seen evidence of that in other rooms as well, and here as there, the workmanship appeared to be very professional.

Finally, he returned to the billiards room, which he could see had been paneled years ago. There was no indication that any of the old woodwork had been tampered with at any time.

He'd come to a dead end. He'd already had ample opportunity to check the converted carriage house and stable and had found nothing there. The only other building on the property was George's cottage, which he had no way to examine.

For possibly the first time in his very inquisitive life, Max decided to allow a mystery to remain unsolved. If Singing Waters held any ugly secrets, they were now safe from him. He felt a vague annoyance at being forced to give up, but that was far outweighed by a sense of relief at not having to face the consequences of any grisly discovery.

But as Max was setting aside his quest for answers, Annelise was just beginning to face her own suspicions. Her thoughts and memories had been building slowly for days, linking past and present, denying and then questioning.

She kept all this to herself, however. Giving voice to her terrible suspicions seemed akin to an act of treason. Max had been quite correct in stating that she idolized Otto; it did indeed come very close to that. His love for her, combined with what she perceived to be her father's rejection of her, had created a bond that persisted long after his death.

Therefore, even as her doubts began to grow, she found herself unable to face them squarely. What happened, finally, was that she crept up on them slowly until there could be no turning back.

One afternoon, while Max was out somewhere on his dirt bike, she decided to engage in what she referred to as one of her periodic "bouts of domesticity." Max had mentioned to her that much of the wine stored in the wine cellar was very old and had probably gone bad. His point had been proven one evening when he had uncorked a bottle whose smell had very nearly driven them both from the kitchen.

So she decided to do an inventory, then consult an expert Max knew to determine which bottles should be kept and which should be consigned to the trash. Since Otto's death and the subsequent death of her father, the wine cellar had fallen into disuse. The older members of the family clung to their special favorites, which they generally brought with them, and the younger generation for the most part favored mineral water or lighter, white wines. The large, multicourse dinners of the past at which many different wines had been consumed had also given way to a lighter, more casual diet.

So, with clipboard in hand, she went off to the wine cellar, where she began to record the vintages. It took quite a while, since there was still quite a supply of bottles. Before long Annelise's thoughts returned to her childhood when she had frequently played in this quiet spot with its delightful, fruity aromas.

She'd been staring at the wall opposite the doorway for some minutes before the thought crept into her mind and then seized it in a chilling grip. The clipboard and pencil just slid from her hands and clattered noisily to the floor as she stared at that wall—the wall that had, at some point, seemed to move closer.

No, she told herself stubbornly. You know perfectly well—and have known for years—that it's only the difference between childish and adult perceptions. The room seems smaller because you've become larger.

But not that much larger, her mind told her. You played down here until you were eight or nine—until about twenty years ago. Until about the time Otto decided that the wine cellar should be kept locked to prevent your older cousins from nipping into the wine—even though they denied having done such a thing.

Involuntarily, she began to move toward the wall. Because of the position of the overhead lights, that wall was the one most in shadow.

At first glance, there was nothing at all different about it. Like the others, it was brick, now dulled with age. Cracks showed in the mortar. But that prickly feeling that had begun in the back of her neck had now spread throughout her body—and would not go away.

She remembered there was a flashlight in the boiler room and flew down the hallway to retrieve it. Then, holding it with both hands in a futile attempt to keep it steady, she began to play it over the wall.

She thought she detected a slight difference in coloration when she compared the bricks in the wall with the others in the room. Even the bright light of the flashlight, however, wasn't strong enough for Annelise to be sure. She dragged a stool over to the wall and climbed up to examine the top. The wine racks ran floor to ceiling, concealing the top of the wall from the view of anyone standing before it.

There was a difference there, too. On the other walls, the bricks had been laid neatly, forming a straight line. But on this wall, the line was uneven, and cement had been used to patch up the mistake.

She got down from the stool shakily, then began to back away toward the door. There she stopped, her heart thudding noisily in her chest. Her spine seemingly encased in ice.

She was still standing there staring at it when she heard the roar of Max's motorcycle in the distance. Her first, purely instinctive reaction was to cover up any evidence of her discovery. So she moved the stool back to its place near the door, switched off the lights and closed the door behind her.

Max knew something was wrong the moment he saw her. She barely acknowledged his kiss and held herself stiffly in his arms. He ran a finger along a smudge on her cheek.

"What were you doing—playing in the dirt?"

"Wha-what do you mean?" she asked nervously.

"You have a streak of dirt on your cheek and you look like a kid who's just been caught doing something she shouldn't."

She moved out of his arms with a brittle attempt at a laugh. "Oh, I was just down in the wine cellar, inventorying the wines. That must be how I got dirty." Then, knowing that her nervousness must be evident, she embroidered upon the truth.

"There was a spider—a really big one. If you hadn't been on that noisy bike, you would have heard me scream all the way out in the woods."

Max looked toward the basement doorway, recalling his own explorations down there and the scurrying things he'd seen in the old root cellar. He wondered if she too might have been exploring. He hugged her and laughed.

"Should I get out my shotgun and go after it?"

But by later that evening, Max was having second thoughts about that spider. He had made a very serious study of this woman he loved, and he knew every small nuance of her behavior. Something had shaken her, something she refused to talk about.

He managed to slip away from her for long enough to make another quick check of the basement, but found nothing. Perhaps, after all, it had only been a spider.

Max knew that although Annelise loved him, she hadn't quite accepted the consequences of that love. Several times during the past few days, he had tried to bring up the subject of their future, and on each occasion, she had deflected the issue. Perhaps he was pushing too hard.

He knew there were problems. She would have to move to Boston, which she claimed to dislike. He knew she also disliked the academic world, into which she would surely be drawn. And most of all, he suspected that down deep inside, she might think of love as being the ultimate invasion of her cherished privacy.

Unconsciously, he drew her closer to him as they sat in the big lounge chair, watching a French film she loved but he thought boring. His French was minimal at best and all the actors seemed to do was talk.

He was tempted to reach for the remote control button and cut off the gibberish, then demand that they talk about the future right here and now. But she appeared to have relaxed somewhat and was obviously deeply engrossed in the film.

Max was wrong. Annelise was barely paying attention to the film. Neither was she giving any thought at all to their future. Her mind was wholly preoccupied with that wall in the wine cellar.

All the scattered dark thoughts that had been flitting about in her mind for days now finally coalesced into one monstrous terror: Otto, her beloved uncle, might well have been a murderer.

That argument she had thought she'd overheard in the library so many years ago now seemed highly plausible. As a child, she'd sensed that her uncle had been lying when he'd told her that what she'd heard had been the stereo; as an adult, she now became chillingly certain that her instincts had been correct.

How or why such a thing could have happened didn't matter now; her entire being was focused on proving or disproving Otto's guilt. Oddly enough, now that the opportunity to do so appeared to be at hand, she felt a calmness come over her. But it was a cold, deadly calm.

The next day, when Max once again went for a ride on his dirt bike, she went to work. First, she removed the remaining bottles from the rack. Then, with great difficulty, she succeeded in moving the rack itself away from the wall. After this had been accomplished, the sloppy nature of the brickwork became more evident. Otto, she knew, had never been much of a handyman.

Finally, she selected a spot in the middle of the wall and began to chip away at the mortar with a heavy chisel she had purloined from George's workshop.

Though the mortar appeared to be loose and even cracked in places, Annelise quickly discovered that brick walls cannot be disassembled easily. She worked at the task doggedly, ignoring the protests of her straining muscles and the blisters that soon formed on her hand. But she had done no more than loosen two sides of one brick when she heard the sound of Max's motorcycle.

She'd foolishly believed that she could complete the work in a few hours and now faced the problem of covering the evidence of her labors. With great effort she pulled the wine rack back to the wall, then hurriedly shoved a few bottles back onto the shelves. The others she left on the floor, assuming that she could come up with some excuse if Max should come down here.

Then she left the wine cellar, rushed up the stairs to the kitchen, and without pausing for breath, dashed up the back staircase to her bedroom. By the time Max came into her bedroom, she had discarded her dusty clothing and was standing under the soothing spray of her shower.

"Do you want some company in there?" he called through the closed door.

She didn't—and she did. She wanted his closeness, but on *her* terms. So she said yes, and a few minutes later, he joined her

168

under the steamy spray, filling the space with his big, familiar body.

"Mmm, that feels good," he said, moving in front of the spray and at the same time sliding his arms around her.

He took the soapy sponge from her and began to wash her and then himself. It took him a while to realize that his own growing desire wasn't matched by hers.

They stepped out of the shower and he wrapped himself in a towel, then took another and began to dry her. "What's wrong?" he asked with gentle concern.

"I . . . have a headache, Max," she lied. "I just want to lie down for a while."

Max thought wryly that she wasn't even lying very originally, but he picked her up and carried her out to the bedroom, where he deposited her gently on the bed.

"Are you sure that's all that's wrong?"

"Yes," she said, closing her eyes to avoid looking at him while she lied.

Tell him, an inner voice commanded. But she ignored it. She would wait until she was sure. She needed only one more day, surely.

Max kissed her softly and left the room. He was now firmly convinced that something was going on that he needed to know about, and that she wasn't going to tell him.

Annelise kept her eyes closed, seeing that brick wall with one loose brick.

CHAPTER ELEVEN

"I'm going out riding for a few hours," Max announced from the doorway of Annelise's studio.

When she straightened up and turned to face him, Max thought he saw a grimace of pain cross her face. He also noted she appeared to have accomplished very little, although she'd spent the entire day thus far working. But he said none of this to her, because he'd already decided that he would have to find out for himself what was troubling her.

As soon as she heard the sound of the motorcycle receding into the distance, Annelise left her studio and went to her room to change into heavier clothing. She'd been hoping that he would decide to go riding, but had been afraid to ask because she knew he suspected that something was wrong.

Barely five minutes later Annelise was back in the wine cellar.

She hesitated only for a moment before striding purposefully to the wine rack and once more removing the bottles. Then she tugged and pushed the wine rack away from the wall again, retrieved the chisel from its hiding place, and set to work once more.

Annelise was driven at this point, driven by a need to prove or disprove her fears. She still believed Otto to have been incapable of violence, but she also believed her own instincts and memories. Working feverishly, she was only barely aware of her exertions.

The first brick that she had loosened the day before came out relatively easily, falsely leading her to believe that others would follow as quickly. But after an hour's work, she had only one more brick out and the others looked formidably solid.

Then, after she had finally managed to remove the third brick, the one above it came loose quite suddenly. Its falling loosened its neighbor and that in turn slightly loosened the one next to that, and in less time than she had expected at this point, Annelise had opened a hole nearly two feet square. The final brick fell backward into the wall and she heard it thud against something that didn't sound like a stone floor.

She backed away quickly, hearing echoes of that dull thud as her mind filled with grisly images. Was she really prepared to face this? Shouldn't she just wait until Max returned and ask him to look? But the hope lingered stubbornly that she was wrong, and if she was, how could she explain to him what she had feared?

So she picked up the flashlight, then felt a wave of dizzying fear and dropped it again. It clattered noisily to the floor, and she took several deep, steadying breaths before she bent to retrieve it. The lens had cracked, but when she switched it on, the light still worked and she approached the hole she'd made, clutching it in both hands.

With a long, ragged breath, Annelise prepared to confront her worst fears. Images of what might lay behind that wall had already flooded into her mind by the time she managed to get both her head and the flashlight through the opening.

It was a long box, crudely nailed together from unfinished wood, and its ugly, familiar shape could not be denied. She stared in horror at it, ignoring the fetid odor and knowing that moment of deadly, cold calmness when dread suspicions become absolute certainty.

Her eyes were blurring with tears by the time she pulled her head back from the opening and once again let the flashlight slip through her fingers. She struck her head painfully against a brick at the top of the hole, and she let out a cry that was cut off sharply as she heard the sound of running footsteps on the basement stairs.

Before she could do anything more than look wildly about her for a way to hide her discovery, Max was there, pausing for only an instant in the doorway before rushing to her and folding her into his arms.

Fear and the dull ache in her head made her dizzy. She didn't protest as Max scooped her up and carried her from the room. But by the time he had gotten her up to the kitchen, some semblance of reason had reasserted itself, and she struggled to be set down.

"In the library," he said as he tightened his grip against her struggles. "You need to lie down."

Her mind had finally focused on the fact that he was here, instead of out riding. When did he return? She should have heard the sound of that motorcycle even in the basement.

"Wha-what are you doing here?" she asked as he lay her down on the sofa.

He ignored her as he tipped her chin up and peered at her eyes. "Is your vision blurred?"

She wiped at the tears that lingered on her lashes. "No. Wha . . . ?"

"That was a bad bump on the head. You could have a concussion."

"I'm fine," she replied in an annoyed tone, knowing that was far from the truth. "Why did you come back so soon?"

"I didn't go anywhere," he said, as though that should explain everything.

"You *said* you were going riding."

"*You* said nothing was wrong," he countered.

"I didn't hear your bike," she went on, trying to postpone the awful truth as long as possible.

"That's because I left it some distance down the road. How did you know where to look?"

She simply stared at him in open-mouthed astonishment.

"I tried to find it myself, but I had no idea where to begin," he went on.

"Find what? How could you possibly have known?" The words rushed out in a torrent as new waves of iciness engulfed her.

"I didn't know—I only guessed."

She closed her eyes, seeing that box again. "It was a box—a handmade coffin."

Max felt some relief at that. At least she'd been spared the sight of some moldering skeleton like he'd half expected to find in the root cellar. But it probably didn't make much difference in the long run. The horror wasn't the body itself; it was what it meant to her.

"Why, Max? Otto wasn't a mur-murderer." She barely uttered the word and then collapsed into great, choking sobs.

Max sat down beside her and took her into his arms. "No, I don't think he was."

But he spoke with more certainty than he felt at the moment. Still, a possible explanation had begun to occur to him, one that didn't leave Otto totally blameless, but didn't make him a murderer either. The need to settle this for her sake as well as for his brought him to his feet. He had just picked up the phone when she rushed at him with a sharp cry.

"No! You can't tell anyone!" she commanded, trying to wrestle the phone from his grasp.

They exchanged stares. His was hurt; hers was angry and insistent. Finally, Max put down the receiver and guided her back to the sofa.

"George already knows, Nellie, and he should be able to tell us the whole truth now."

"George?" she echoed weakly. "But how . . . ?"

"Just let me call him and I'll explain while we wait."

He half expected her to try to stop him again, but she sat quietly on the sofa, her arms wrapped about herself, her fearful eyes on him as he made the call. After he had summoned George, Max sat down beside her and told her all he knew. She said nothing. Her eyes looked huge in her pale, dust-streaked face but she remained absolutely still.

"How did you know where to look?" he asked again when he had finished his story.

By the time she had completed a rambling, sometimes nearly incoherent story of her childhood memories, George had appeared. He looked from Annelise to Max, then back to Annelise again.

"What's happened, Nellie?"

But it was Max who answered as she just continued to sit there, her gaze far away, her thoughts as confused as her words had been. As Max explained, George moved heavily to a chair, then sank into it.

"Nellie," the caretaker said in a voice made gruff with emotion, "Otto didn't kill him—at least not deliberately. He was only trying to disarm the man, and the gun went off. He died instantly."

Max thrust some cognac at her, but she pushed it away as she tried to understand George's words. She didn't even hear Max's next question.

"At first, he was too stunned to think clearly. Then he knew the others would be back soon, so he called me. We decided to hide the body in the old root cellar to give us some time to decide what to do. You see, it happened the evening before all the others were leaving. Everyone else was out at a party and Otto was at home with the children."

George turned his attention back to Annelise. "Otto told me that he decided during the night that he would have to call in the police, regardless of the outcome. But the next morning, he found out that you'd been hiding in the staircase during the storm and had heard the argument.

"He said he knew then he had to cover it up. So he told you that all you'd heard was his opera music. He didn't want you to be hurt by it, and I suppose he must have worried too about what you'd think of him, even though he was innocent."

"But I never really believed that story. I knew it wasn't his music. Instead, I just buried the memory. But it came back when I showed Max the hidden staircase."

"Anyway," George continued, "we decided to bury the man here. I had hidden his car behind the garage the night before, and then I drove it down to Manhattan the next day after everyone had left."

"But why the wine cellar?" Max asked.

"Well, Otto had discovered that the one wall was in need of repair and I'd planned to get someone to do it after the family left. So he decided to put him in there and do the work himself. In fact, he sent Mary and me away as soon as I got back from New York because he didn't want me to be involved. But I would have helped him. Otto was a good friend, and I know that that man's death was just a tragic accident."

George turned imploringly to Annelise, who sat looking from one man to the other, her eyes huge and dark with shock. "Otto was a good man, Nellie. What happened wasn't his fault. It *was* wrong of him to have covered it up, but he did it for the best of reasons. He was already worried about the family's reputation, and then when he realized what it could do to you, that cinched it."

Max was watching Annelise carefully as the caretaker talked to her. He still had plenty of questions for the man, but they could wait. She was deathly pale and her gaze seemed unfocused. But Max thought that if anything at all could be salvaged for her from this ungodly mess, it was the certainty that Otto had loved her very much—enough to have gone against what Max knew must have been strong principles. George's next words confirmed that.

"Otto went through a very bad time afterward. He even had your father hire a private detective to make sure that the man hadn't left any dependents. But there weren't—"

"My *father* knew?" Annelise's voice cracked with shock as she stared at George.

George nodded. "Paul and your father came up here that fall for Otto's birthday, and they could tell right away that something was wrong. But Otto and I both kept quiet. Then, a few weeks later, your father came back alone, and that's when Otto told him."

"But Father and Otto didn't even get along. Why would Otto have told him? Why not Paul or even Hilde?"

"Your father backed Otto against a wall, so to speak—and you know how he could be. I think he caught Otto in a weak moment. Besides, since Otto had more or less given his role as head of the family to your father, I think he felt he *had* to be told. As far as I know, none of the others ever knew a thing.

"John agreed that the effect on you would have been very bad, and I suppose he must have been thinking about the family's name, too. So he went along with it."

Annelise had retreated into stillness again as she struggled to assimilate all this. It was too much. Her father and Otto, conspiring to keep a terrible secret because of her. And Singing Waters itself, concealing from her things she had never quite forgotten, tormenting her with clues, but withholding the truth all these years.

Max sat down beside her, wanting to draw her into his arms. But he felt her resistance even before he could make the attempt, so he settled instead for holding her hand.

"You have to decide what's to be done now, Nellie," he said gently.

She looked at him as though he were a stranger suddenly come into their midst. Max's heart knotted painfully, but he did not release her hand.

She stared down at those intertwined hands for a moment, then nodded slowly.

"Paul must be told," she said finally. "I'll call him."

Max let her go and she got up somewhat shakily, then before his admiring eyes drew upon her considerable strength and walked over to pick up the phone. Apparently, she was told that Paul was unavailable, because Max heard the return of that imperious tone she'd used on him that first day.

"This is Annelise and I must talk to him—*now!*"

Apparently, it worked, because a moment later, she was talking to Paul.

Max stood unobtrusively in a corner of the library, directly in front of the bookcase that hid the stairwell. Night had fallen on Singing Waters and with it had come Paul, Hilde, and Rowan. Paul sat at Otto's desk, his expression grave. Hilde and Annelise were like rigid mirror images on the sofa. Rowan and George sat in nearby chairs.

In spite of his continued concern for Annelise, Max found the tableau fascinating. These people had all received what had to be the greatest shock of their lives, and yet that ineffable dignity remained intact.

In the interim between George's admission and the arrival of the others, Annelise had behaved as though Max were invisible. Even before she left to spend most of that time out in the woods, she had withdrawn to some place where he couldn't follow.

Max had already gotten from George the answers he'd sought, and now Paul was asking the same question: Why?

George had told him that Otto had been surprised at Harrington's unexpected arrival, then shocked when Harrington had virtually demanded that Otto turn over to him the work in which Harrington himself had played no part at all. The two had apparently met at some scientific gathering, and then had corresponded after that.

George's story had confirmed what Max knew Harrington's fellow faculty members had suspected: Harrington had been a man obsessed. His work to that point had been inferior and he must have known that he would not receive tenure. So he had apparently decided to steal what he could not produce.

Otto had quite naturally refused to turn it over. Harrington had then produced a gun, and the two men had struggled over it. Then, with Harrington dead, Otto had thought it best to lie about his work so no one would ever suspect Harrington would have been interested in it.

Otto had never told George what he'd done with the work, and George, with little interest in such things, had never thought to ask.

Otto's decision to hide it years later in a place where only Annelise would be likely to find it made a strange, if terrible, kind of sense. It had been because of her that he had concealed it, so he had in the end bequeathed it to her—although he'd had no way of knowing that its discovery would start a chain of events that would reveal what had happened that stormy night. Or perhaps he had actually wanted her to know the truth one day. They would never know.

Max turned his attention back to the others as Paul finally spoke into the heavy silence that had followed George's description of those events.

"I think, Nellie, that it's really up to you to decide what's to be done now."

"Me?" she asked in a choked voice. "Why me?"

"Because it was for you that Otto and your father kept this secret."

Max watched her as she sat there with her head bowed, looking so heartwrenchingly fragile. But he couldn't go to her. He loved her now from what seemed a very great distance.

Then, suddenly, she looked directly at him. Max felt a momentary exhilaration, as though he'd just been returned from invisibility.

"Max could publish Otto's work as his own," she said, speaking to the others, but focusing only on him. "And no one need ever know about . . . the rest of it."

Max knew that this was what she wanted, but he was already shaking his head.

"No, Nellie. That wouldn't be fair. It was Otto's work and he deserves credit for it." He took a deep breath and forged on.

"And if the truth is going to come out, it should be the *whole* truth."

He felt the agreement of the others, but knew that Annelise didn't yet share it. She was silent for a moment, then got up.

"I . . . I have to think about it."

They all watched her as she left the room. Max knew that she had withdrawn from him again if indeed she had ever actually returned. He cursed himself briefly for not having given in to her solution, but knew that he just couldn't do it. She didn't understand that to claim another man's work as his own—for whatever reason—was something he just couldn't live with.

Paul Vandeveldt got up and came over to Max, placing a hand on his shoulder.

"You're right, Max. She'll see that sooner or later."

Max glanced from Paul to the others and saw their silent agreement. Then he saw something more. With that simple gesture, Paul had signaled to Max that he was now a part of this powerful, close-knit family. He understood, finally, what Rowan had meant when he'd said that money wasn't important. Acceptance was based on what a man believed and not who he was. Max had just been accepted—by all but one of them, at any rate.

Annelise stopped by the lake's edge, then sank down onto the grassy bank. Her anger with Max over his refusal to cooperate had already begun to wane. She didn't yet fully understand why he had refused her, but she knew that it stemmed from his basic decency and sense of honor.

Somewhat surprisingly, her thoughts continued to center not on Otto and the dilemma he had bequeathed to her but on Max. At first, she thought that he had backed away from her, abandoning her just when she needed him most. But then the doubts began to creep in. Had *she* been the one to turn away? She wasn't sure.

What should she do about this terrible discovery? She couldn't really be angry with the others for having put this burden on her, although she had secretly hoped that they would make the decision for her.

It occurred to her as she sat there that this was the first time she had ever been forced to become a responsible, adult member of the family. She'd left childhood behind years ago, but its aura had lingered and she'd done nothing to dispel it. Paul managed her finances, Hilde tried her best to manage her personal life—and even her father and Otto had protected her long after she should have been told the truth. Furthermore, she'd allowed this to happen because she had wanted no part of being a Vandeveldt.

A twenty-eight-year rebellion was drawing to a close. It was time, they were telling her, for her to stop setting herself apart.

Max started down to the lake when he saw her sitting there in the spot where they'd once made love. He had no idea what he was going to say to her or what her attitude toward him might be at this moment, but he was feeling that incredible magnetism that had first drawn him to this elusive woman. He loved her and he needed her, too. But at the moment, he just wasn't sure that she was willing to meet that need.

She must have heard his approach, because she turned her head slightly in his direction, sending that black and white mane swinging across her shoulders as it glistened in the pale moonlight.

Without a word, Max sat down behind her, then cradled her between his long legs and drew her back against his chest. She tucked her head beneath his chin and relaxed against him. They both stared in silence at the dark, shimmering lake. Behind them, the lights from the house cast a golden glow.

"It must have been terrible for Otto and Father to have carried around that secret all those years," she said into the silence that followed a loon's hysterical cry.

"Yes," he agreed. "And for Otto to have kept his work hidden. It *is* important work, Nellie. The more I pursue it, the more I can see that. I think that Otto might one day become a historic figure in physics. If his work is published, that is."

"But you already know about it," she said, thinking back to that lunchtime conversation with Paul. "Whether or not it's actually published, you already have that knowledge."

Max was silent for a moment, and then nodded his agreement. "Yes, but I wouldn't feel right about using it without giving him credit."

"You're making this decision very difficult for me, Max."

"I know that."

Another silence fell between them. Max waited. He knew her well enough to know what she would eventually decide. All that remained was to give her time.

Finally, she moved away from him and got to her feet. "I'm going up to tell them."

"Tell them what?" he asked, standing up as well.

"You already know what I'm going to tell them. I think you've known all along."

Her tone wasn't really accusatory, but Max thought he sensed just the smallest bit of annoyance. It wasn't the first time he'd known her mind before she herself had, and it wasn't the first time she had spoken to him like that, either.

Max followed her back to the library. All the others were still there, and several conversations broke off abruptly as she entered.

"I think the truth must be told," she stated firmly. "All of it."

Paul nodded and smiled briefly at both Annelise and Max. The others murmured their agreement.

"I'll get our legal team and p.r. people up here now, and we'll call in the authorities in the morning," Paul said. "Max, I'm sure they'll want to talk to your department head and anyone else who might be able to reconfirm that Harrington was mentally unstable. With their testimony and George's, there's no doubt about the results of any inquiry. Even the gun that George says was buried with Harrington may be able to be traced back to him."

Paul continued to address Max. "After that, it's up to you to handle the release of Otto's papers. I guess I'd be less than candid if I didn't say that I hope they'll cause quite a stir in the scientific community."

"They will," Max assured him.

"And speaking as head of the family, I'd like to tell you that we're going to establish a research chair in Otto's name at MIT. Would it be reasonable to assume that you might occupy that chair?"

Max was somewhat flustered. "Well, it *is* my research area, but—"

"Well, that decision will be up to your department head, of course," Paul put in quickly. "But it seems appropriate to me. You and Otto would have gotten along well. You seem to have had at least two interests in common."

Max nodded as he looked down at the figure beside him. He was very worried about his future with one of those "interests."

CHAPTER TWELVE

The rest of that night and the following day saw a flurry of activity that was distinctly at odds with the tranquillity of Singing Waters.

Five lawyers arrived shortly after midnight, accompanied by a man who handled the family's public relations. Paul's personal assistant arrived by a separate flight from Boston. The big house hummed with activity well into the night.

The younger generation of Vandeveldts were called, and two of them, including Annelise's brother, were there by early morning. Both were almost excessively curious about Max, who privately agreed with Annelise's earlier, somewhat scathing assessment of them.

Max was bemused by the differences between the way ordinary families handled such crises, and the way they were dealt with by a family such as this. If before he'd had an incomplete understanding of the term "cushioned by wealth," he certainly understood it now. He wondered with considerable amusement how the local authorities would deal with all this high-priced talent.

Through it all, he and Annelise seemed to be moving in separate orbits. Together with Rowan and George, Max went down to the wine cellar to see just how much work would be involved in removing the makeshift coffin from the wall. Max, who had not seen Annelise for some time, turned to find her standing in the doorway of the wine cellar, staring at the hole she had created.

Leaving the other two men to their discussion of brickwork,

Max went to her and folded her into his arms. She didn't resist, but she did no more than allow herself to be held for a few minutes before pulling away. Max stood there in the hallway and watched her walk back up the stairs, a slim, erect figure whose continued remoteness gnawed at his very soul.

Several hours later, after the others began to arrive, Max went off to bed, to a room he hadn't used for many weeks. Once more, he felt like a stranger in the house.

For a long time, he lay awake, hoping against hope that she might join him. But when he finally fell asleep, he was still alone in bed.

Max and Annelise stood side by side, watching the departure of the final contingent of visitors: Paul, Hilde, and Rowan. All the others had left shortly before and the house behind them was silent.

The coffin had been removed, and George was already at work on the wall. Lawyers and police had clashed politely and a hearing date would soon be announced. The public relations man had left first of all, to handle his end of it from Manhattan. Before he departed, he had spoken by phone with the president of MIT, who would soon announce the receipt of Otto Vandeveldt's papers, as well as the endowment of a research chair in his name.

While all this was happening, Max had reached a decision and made a call himself. Now, as the station wagon carrying the last of the visitors disappeared over the crest of the hill, he took Annelise's hand in his.

"I'm leaving, too. I've already packed."

At first, she just stared at him curiously, as though he were speaking a language she didn't quite understand. Then she pulled her hand from his and backed away a few steps.

"Why?"

"Because it's necessary. I'm leaving for Spain in a few days to go caving."

"It's necessary for you to go caving?" she asked, sounding incredulous.

Max shook his head. "No, it's just necessary for me to leave. Going caving is just a diversion."

"A diversion from what?" she asked in a tone that hinted at understanding.

"A diversion while I wait for you to decide about us."

"I don't want you to go, Max."

"Perhaps not, but I don't think you really know if you want me to stay, either—except on your terms."

"*My* terms?" she echoed.

"Yes. Your terms that I just can't accept."

"I don't know what you're talking about, Max."

"I'm talking about trust, Nellie. That's what's been missing here. You didn't trust me enough to give me Otto's papers until I confronted you. You didn't trust me enough to talk over your suspicions with me. Then you didn't even trust me enough to know that I wouldn't have taken any action without talking it over with you. When I picked up the phone to call George, you thought I was going to call the police.

"And there's also a matter of need. When people love, they also *need.* I needed to comfort you and to be there for you, but you wouldn't let me because you didn't need me."

"But I *did* need you and I still do."

"Then you're not very good at communicating that," Max stated bluntly. "I've tried to give you the space you need, but all that's happened is that you've withdrawn from me."

"Do you still love me?"

"Of course, but I also want to know that you love me enough to need me—not just part of the time, but all the time."

Max didn't know what to expect as she stood there staring at him. There might have been a certain masculine pleasure to be gained if she had thrown herself into his arms and begged him to stay, but he'd never expected that to happen. Annelise Vandeveldt would never beg.

185

"How am I supposed to prove that to you?" she demanded defiantly.

He looked at her steadily. "If you feel it, you'll be able to prove it to me."

She searched his face with a disconcerting intensity, then finally nodded. Max carefully restrained himself from taking her into his arms and went instead to get his bags. She was still standing there when he had carried the last of them to his van.

She stared at the empty trailer hitch. "What about your motorcycle?"

"I'm leaving it here as collateral," Max said with a smile.

"Collateral?" she asked, almost smiling herself.

"Against a loan. I'm lending you yourself for a while. When I come back to get it, the loan comes due."

"That's a very strange sort of loan."

"You can be a very strange sort of woman," he replied. "I saw that from the very beginning."

Now she *did* laugh—and ran into his arms just as he had hoped she would. He held her and caressed her and felt desire stirring through them both. The caves of the Basque country seemed light-years away. But he gave her one last kiss and then firmly set her apart.

His last glimpse of Singing Waters included a small figure standing before the fountain, her striking hair billowing in the breeze.

Annelise worked steadily at her easel as the sunlight poured in through the big skylights of her SoHo loft. She had left Singing Waters the day after Max's departure because it suddenly seemed too big and too empty.

Many of her artist friends spoke glowingly of art as self-therapy, but Annelise had never felt that. She'd never been able to set brush to canvas when she was troubled. Never until now. This particular painting was indeed therapy.

Two weeks had passed since Max's abrupt departure from her

186

life, and another two weeks remained before his scheduled return. Those days and nights had seemed both the longest and shortest she'd ever spent. She missed him terribly, but his presence lingered in her mind with such startling clarity that it almost seemed as though he were still with her.

At first, she'd told herself that he simply didn't understand her need for space, for freedom. But then she realized that he *had* understood that—instinctively and from the very beginning. That was surely one of the things she loved best about him.

Then she thought that perhaps he had gone in order to give her time to sort out all the details of their future—for there were surely many that needed to be sorted out. She would have to move to Boston—a city she disliked—because not even a Vandeveldt could bring MIT to Manhattan.

She would have to tolerate the intolerable academic world—to some extent, at least. She was sure a man like Max must have at least some friends outside that world.

But most of all, she would have to deal with the unsettling notion of having someone in her life *all* the time. At first, that didn't sound very appealing to her, regardless of her love for him. But then she started to consider the alternative. Either she wanted Max in her life all the time, or she would not have him in her life at all. That was the unspoken challenge he had issued.

She continued to work and think about it, and with each stroke of the brush, the answer became more and more clear. The day she finished the painting, she had also finished her thinking.

Max rubbed his stubbly face and thought longingly about the comforts that awaited him at the inn. For two days, they had followed the tortuous course of an underground stream, emerging at last near the base of a hill above the village.

His friends were joking and talking and reliving the experience, and Max gamely joined in, although his thoughts were elsewhere. One of the group, who had met Annelise in Boston, had lost no time informing the others that Max was probably on his last caving trip, since he'd fallen in love with a "gorgeous heiress."

Max had pointed out the fact that two others in their group were married, but he'd been shouted down with remarks about how he would henceforth be spending his summers at that wilderness palace he'd told them about, or out on a yacht somewhere.

He hadn't minded the kidding because it had served somehow to make him feel closer to her. And, although he wouldn't admit it to his friends, the truth was that he might not be doing this again. Annelise had become an adventure far more exciting than mere caves or mountains.

As they all trudged wearily into the village, he took in the rugged beauty of this wild, ancient country whose inhabitants were neither French nor Spanish, but defiantly a group apart, and thought that she would like it here, too. Perhaps one day, he would bring her here.

They walked into the small inn to find the place completely empty. It was siesta time. Not even the inn's owner was anywhere about.

Max slipped his key into the lock as he told his friends he would meet them after they had all showered and shaved. Then he pushed the door open, still half-lost in a fantasy that she would be waiting for him.

His jaw dropped and he froze on the threshold. Then he hurriedly glanced behind him to make sure his friends had gone on to their rooms. After that, he closed the door very quickly.

There, propped ostentatiously on a chair in the center of the room, was a painting—a very familiar painting. Actually, the painting wasn't familiar—but the subject certainly was.

He walked gingerly toward it, then bent to examine it more closely. She really was very good—especially with the details. He could even see that small scar along the bottom of his rib cage, the result of a mishap in a cave several years ago.

Then he straightened up and glanced around the room. Had she sent this to him? She must have, because he didn't see any

188

other sign of her presence. He groaned aloud as he thought about the leers he was going to receive from whoever had carried this up here.

He went back to the painting again, wondering how long it had taken her to complete it and what she'd been thinking about while she worked on it. He knew damned well what *he* would have been thinking about if he'd done a nude painting of her.

It wasn't until he went to the big wardrobe in the corner that he found her luggage, together with the tube that had held the canvas.

Totally forgetting about his unsavory appearance, Max bounded down the stairs of the inn to find the proprietor was now back at his desk.

"Ah, Professor Armstrong. You are pleased with your surprise —no?"

Max wasn't sure just what the man meant, but he hoped fervently that it wasn't the painting. He also belatedly remembered that he hadn't locked his door.

"Where is she? When did she arrive?"

"A few hours ago. Your wife is a most unusual woman. Very beautiful."

Max grinned and thanked the man. This was a very conservative village, so he didn't bother to tell him that it was a bit premature to call Annelise his wife. He had no intention of sleeping alone this night.

"Do you know where she is now?" he asked eagerly.

"I saw her a little while ago, walking through the village."

He hurried out the door, then turned in the opposite direction from which they had just come. The streets were nearly empty and he had no problem spotting her. Not that he would have had in any event, he thought, and grinned.

She was seated on a low stone wall near an old church, her big sketchpad propped up against her bent knees, and she was so intent upon her work that she didn't even see him approaching. Ignoring for the moment the temptation to toss her sketchpad aside and sweep her into his arms, Max bent to bestow a chaste kiss to her brow the moment she looked up and saw him.

"What kind of kiss is that, for someone you haven't seen for three weeks?" she asked with a smile.

"Three weeks and one day," he corrected. "And that was a husbandly kiss."

She laughed. "Well, I'm sure this place must be very old-fashioned, so how else could I have gotten a key to your room?"

"You might have said you were my sister," he suggested.

"Right," she said mockingly as she closed her sketchpad and slid the pencil into its holder. "We certainly look like brother and sister."

"Do we look like husband and wife?"

She regarded him steadily for a long moment. "Yes, I think we do. What do you think?"

"I've thought that for some time. I was just waiting for you to agree with me."

"I'm not very easy to live with, you know," she went on.

"No!" he exclaimed, feigning great shock. "I never would have guessed."

She laughed, and then gradually grew very serious. "But I *do* need you, Max, even if I haven't really proved that."

"Well, as long as you promise to work on it, I'm willing to give you a chance," he said with a smile.

"It may take a while," she warned.

"I'm a very patient man," he said as he took the sketchpad from her, set it aside, then drew her into his arms.

"That's why I'm marrying you," she said as she caressed his beard-roughened cheek.

Max bent to kiss her very gently, aware of the damage his unshaven face could do to her soft skin. But she pulled him closer, then arched herself to him with a soft moan of surrender.

"It's a pity my room doesn't come equipped with a Jacuzzi," he said regretfully.

"But it does have a fireplace," she reminded him. "And I imagine the nights can be quite cool here in the mountains."

They walked slowly back to the inn, arms about each other's waists.

"Have you been to your room yet?" she asked as they ascended the stairs of the inn. "Or did the owner tell you I was here?"

"Yes, I've been to my room," he said, remembering again that he'd left it unlocked.

"And?"

"It's, ah, very good. You didn't even miss the scar."

"I don't think I missed anything," she stated wickedly. "Although I'll need to check to make sure."

"I'll be happy to accommodate—" Max stopped abruptly as they reached the upstairs hallway and he saw his friends crowded around his open door.

She smiled broadly. "How nice. My very first one-woman show."

Max reminded himself that he'd known all along that life with her would never be dull.